Mahin was born and raised in Portland, Oregon. She's been writing since she was a child. *BadLands* was written when she was 15. This is her first novel. You can find her drowned in a book or watching *Lord of the Rings* religiously.

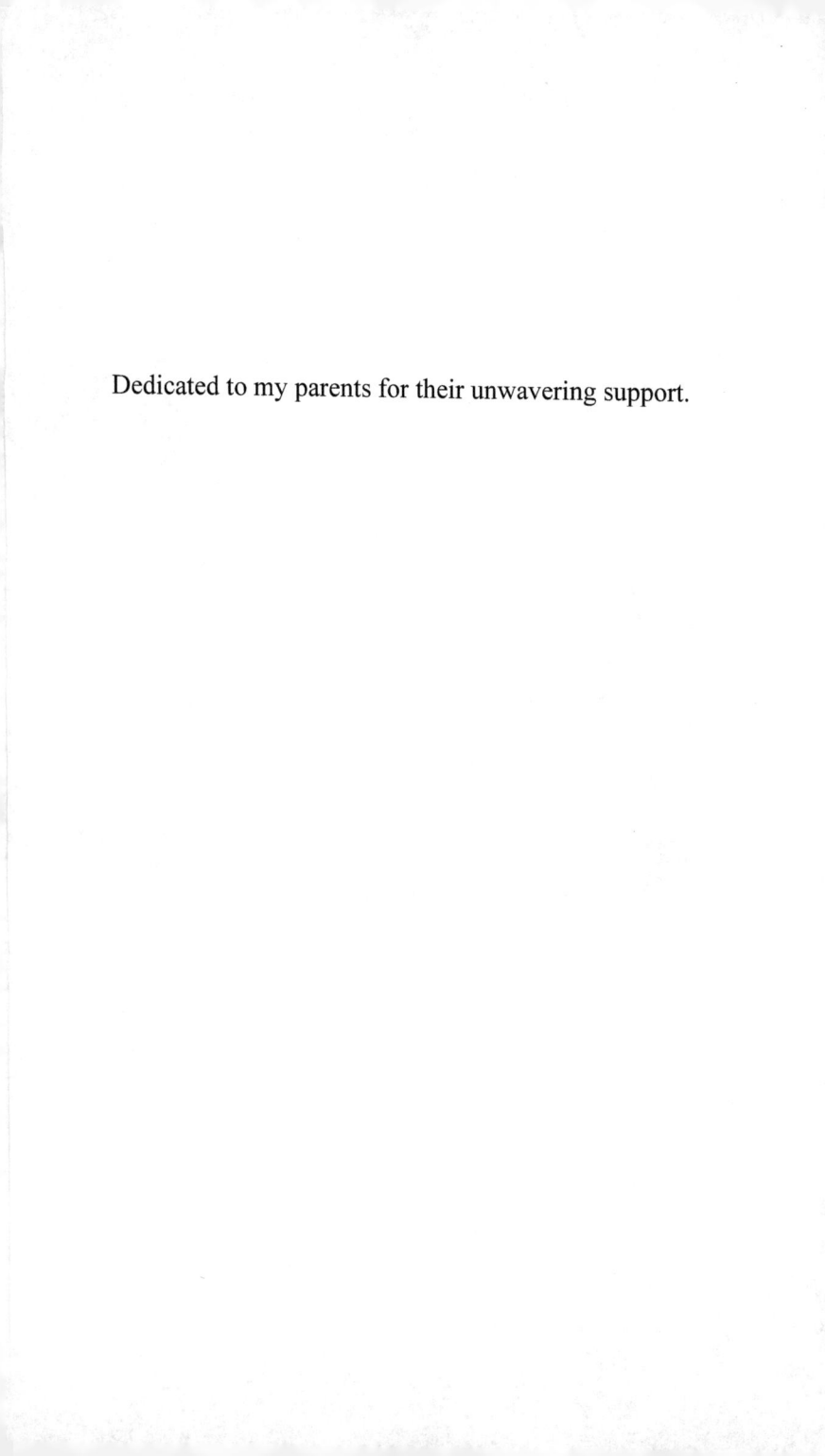

Dedicated to my parents for their unwavering support.

Mahin Mughal

BADLANDS

Love Can't Be Forced

AUSTIN MACAULEY PUBLISHERS™
LONDON • CAMBRIDGE • NEW YORK • SHARJAH

Copyright © Mahin Mughal (2019)

All rights reserved. No part of this publication may be reproduced, distributed, or transmitted in any form or by any means, including photocopying, recording, or other electronic or mechanical methods, without the prior written permission of the publisher, except in the case of brief quotations embodied in critical reviews and certain other non-commercial uses permitted by copyright law. For permission requests, write to the publisher.

Any person who commits any unauthorized act in relation to this publication may be liable to criminal prosecution and civil claims for damages.

Ordering Information:
Quantity sales: special discounts are available on quantity purchases by corporations, associations, and others. For details, contact the publisher at the address below.

Publisher's Cataloging-in-Publication data
Mughal, Mahin
BadLands: Love Can't Be Forced

ISBN 9781641829052 (Paperback)
ISBN 9781641829069 (Hardback)
ISBN 9781645366386 (ePub e-book)

The main category of the book — Young Adult Fiction / Romance / Contemporary

www.austinmacauley.com/us

First Published (2019)
Austin Macauley Publishers LLC
40 Wall Street, 28th Floor
New York, NY 10005
USA

mail-usa@austinmacauley.com
+1 (646) 5125767

I want to thank my mom and dad for their constant support and encouragement. Thanks Dad for convincing me to query editors in the first place. I would like to thank Nikki for always replying to my quite annoying emails and I want to thank the staff at Austin Macauley for helping me bring my dream to life.

Prologue

He wasn't answering.

I glanced at the number of messages left, and still, no response. I could feel my fingers beginning to shake as they glazed across his contact name in bright letters, and I released a breath I never realized I was holding. Liz told me to call the police and I did. I couldn't keep it to myself anymore.

God damn it. Where was he? *I don't know where he is.* I realized the sound of my heart rate increasing was a sign that I knew something utterly terrible was happening, but I couldn't pinpoint exactly *what*, and that was by far the worst feeling imaginable. I suddenly felt the world was spinning on an entirely different axis as the numerous police cars came into view; the sound of a police car the only thing I could hear. I didn't understand what came over me; I hadn't a single idea of what was going on, but I felt like I *knew*.

So, when the police entered my house without warning, I choked back a sob because the sheer sight of them worried me. *Where was he?* I started to move away to the corner of the room, lowering my body on the surface of the wood and yanking my phone out. I was crying before I realized it.

I hated this. I hated not knowing. I felt sick, wanting to throw up. I held my stomach. In a way, I was trying to hold myself together.

Eight days since our last texts. He read my message but never replied back. Everything flew into my head, the parties, the dates, the dinners, and it was then when I realized my head knew exactly what was happening but my heart refused to believe it. My fingers glossed across the texts messages, just as my head ached with a new pain that was unrecognizable.

I didn't understand.

It wasn't like this was the first time Flynn had been off the map; he had run away so many times that it almost felt normal. He never did anything like this when he was with me—was. *Was. Was.* The use of the word in the past sent an instant red sign to my chest. A *mess*. This is a mess. I was a mess. He was a mess. *This wasn't right.*

I guess the policeman understood something, because in an instant, he was racing up the sidewalk, pushing the front door open, and bombarding me with questions I had no response to. And that only scared me more because Flynn was someone I thought I knew, but maybe I didn't. Maybe I *never* knew. Maybe I created fake promises and fake people in my head to replace the true beings. Or maybe he simply never bothered to show me himself. All these months, I never truly knew him. And that hurt more than the idea of him being gone. Because he always was. Gone, gone, gone—my mind chanted as the policeman snapped his fingers in front of me in an effort to regain my attention, but maybe I was gone too.

"When was the last time you saw 18-year-old Flynn Johnson?" The police guy had an intent look in his eyes, his hand gripping a pen as he held a notebook in his other hand. He sighed.

"Henr—"

I couldn't look at him as I uttered my next words.

"*I don't know*. A week ago, I think. Maybe."

"*Maybe*? You're his girlfriend, correct?"

Girlfriend.

"Um..." I started, my voice drifting off into a mere whisper, and I hugged myself like I was cold, but only, I wasn't. *I was alone.* "Yes." The one word was supposed to roll off my tongue so smoothly, *yes, yes, yes, I was his girlfriend*, but it didn't feel like that and that wasn't right. I *should* know where he is. I *should* be there for him. I *should* understand him. Know him in ways he didn't. But I didn't. So I turned my body and started walking towards the front door, but the policeman caught up to me, his fingers gently brushing across the fabric of my tee.

"What's his house address?" And then, I suddenly placed a hand to my mouth, covering the loud gasp as I hurriedly grabbed my car keys and ran off towards my car, leaving the man at my door with no response. *What was happening?*

I didn't understand. I didn't get anything. I couldn't tell myself that that was true, it couldn't be. It doesn't make sense.

Oh God. My mind went into a whirl and I bit back a series of uncontrollable sobs that I knew would eventually crawl down my cheeks. I ignored my dad, my mom, my sister, and I just ran, and the entire time, I prayed I wasn't right. He's not gone, I told myself. He wouldn't do that. He wouldn't do that to himself. To me. To *us.*

And then, in the back of my head, she whispered, *there hardly was*, and I couldn't even shake my head. In this state, I knew it wasn't even safe I was on the road, but I had to get to the barn before the police did. I racked my brain for the address as my fingers dug into the leather material of the steering wheel. Fuck, fuck, fuck, and then my eyes caught the smoke filling the sky behind his house, and it was *all I could see.*

Suddenly, everything froze.

I couldn't move, couldn't *breathe*, but only stared as the blue skies turned into a gray. And then, I was running—running towards the side of his house and forcefully pushing the backyard gate open as tears finally spilled across my lashes. I fell apart, as if my body was no longer in control of my actions. I couldn't feel *anything*.

I don't think I really wanted to.

"*Flynn*! Flynn!" I covered my mouth, blocking the smoke as much as I could. And there I saw, in the corner of my eyes, Flynn's dad's wheelchair broken in two, and his body laying still beside it, his eyes were open but his skin was pale. I couldn't look at him. I couldn't think about what happened.

I could only think about *him.*

I tried to race around the barn, figuring out ways to enter. I couldn't see anything—everything was a dark black—until his curly hair came into view. He was here. *I was alone*. But he was here.

And then, I was falling to the ground; my trembling fingers snaking around his shoulders as I pulled and pulled him further and further from the burning barn. It was so hot. So dark. But I could still make out the pills surrounding his body.

"You're making a fucking mistake," I cried, gripping his left arm as forcefully as I could muster. I sucked in a harsh breath as my nails scratched into his white skin. It felt as if the only air I was breathing in was filled with utter poison; not that I really could breathe in anything.

Only mere seconds before, I couldn't see his chest rise up and down. Only seconds for me to feel the beat of his heart slow down, until it completely stopped and his body was perfectly and utterly still. *No. No. No*. I bent down, my fingers winding around his head as I furiously shook him. Over and over and over. I pressed at his stomach, his face, praying for a sound.

And then his eyes snapped open. And then he was begging for breath. His eyes grew as he grabbed my head, pulling me down towards him, but only, it wasn't *him*. It didn't feel like him; his hands pressed against mine, but the touch felt different, felt fake; didn't look like him, because this boy lying in ashes in front of me, wasn't *my* Flynn. He was a *stranger.*

"Ria," he spluttered, coughing as blood came out from his nose and my sobs became the only sound I could make out.

Part One

Chapter One
7 Months Earlier

My fingers were notched firmly beneath the curtain and the window.

"Where the fuck are you going? It's like 2 a.m.?" I carefully closed the curtain, screwing my eyes shut, before taking in a breath as I turned to face Elaine standing against my doorframe with raised brows.

I wanted to laugh, but then decided against it. She just couldn't leave me be. Why couldn't I do anything without her opinion dangling beside my head?

"Nowhere, now," I muttered, shooting her a glare as I tore my shoes off my feet in an attempt to show her that, in this second, I wasn't leaving. Not yet anyway.

"I was just going out with Margi. I mean, if you're actually at dinner, then you would know she's visiting for the weekend from uni." Elaine's eyes turned considerably dark as she uncrossed her arms and stepped into my room, and I watched as she shut the door.

"Family dinners? *Family? Dinners?*" Her voice felt like a blade. I hated it. I didn't want to talk about it anymore. I really just didn't want to talk to *her* anymore.

"You know, Elaine, they try. Mom tries. Dad tries." I start, but she rolled her eyes and bit down on her lip. I've repeated those words so many times, now they just slip out with no meaning. I just need to keep saying them, that they're *trying*. And trying is more than nothing. But as I keep saying them, it's as if they lose purpose and are just there to replace whatever the truth is.

"They don't fucking *try*. They put that facade on."

"Do you even know what *facad*e means?"

She pursed her lips in a way she did when she wanted to say something but she knew better to say it.

"Just let me go," I said. A lodge in my throat—was I about to cry? *No. Not now.*

Elaine's face started to fall. It was working.

"I don't want to be here right now," I continued, slipping my finger under the window and waving out to Lizzie's car.

"You can't just keep running away," Elaine murmured quietly, beginning to back away towards my room door. Her words went right through me. She just didn't, ever, understand. She never got it. She never got the rush I felt leaving. The excitement of finally being away, away from this house, away from this family.

I mean, deep down, I always knew Elaine was right. Leaving is never a solution, but it felt like one. It felt like a solution for a little bit and a little bit was all I wanted.

I turned back only for a brief second, my eyes boring into hers. I tried to read her but she was putting up a guard.

"Watch me." As I said the words, my lips curled upwards into the smallest of smirks, and before I knew it, I was jumping out of the window and racing towards Lizzie's car. I can keep running. It's all I know, considering it is all I ever do.

"Riaaaaaaaaaaaaaaa. We're gonna go into the city, probably won't be home for a bit!" Liz shouted as I got closer to her car.

"Don't care when we get back," I muttered, not realizing the terrible way it sounded coming off my tongue, but Liz simply shrugged, wrapped her arms around her boyfriend's shoulders, and pushed open the backseat car door for me.

I didn't *want t*o go back. I wanted to stay out. To forget and to pretend. I loved it.

I glanced back at my window and fucking Elaine still stood there; her arms crossed over her chest, but her eyes, which normally gave her feelings and thoughts away, were unreadable. She blinked and closed her eyes, as if she was disappointed in me, before closing the window curtain off. I watched the light dim in the halls before Liz drove off down the road; 'CLOSER' playing on the radio.

Jon, Liz's on-and-off-again boyfriend, tried to switch the radio off, but Liz slapped his hands off the button and I watched as Jon's cheeks reddened and he shamelessly turned to face the window.

This is exactly why they are an on-and-off-again relationship.

"You know what's so weird is we have been riding down this road since we were little kids, babies even," Jon blurted, and I found myself glancing outside as the dead malls, old apartments, and swimming center I used to take swim lessons all passed by.

I started to think about Mom and Dad, and I couldn't stop and I hated it. *I think about them more then they think about me.*

"Like, nothing's changed," Jon continued.

"But we have," Liz said quietly, like the things meant three different things to her than it did to us. I found myself thinking after that, the town just stayed the same. Buildings weren't destroyed, they simply got older. The swim recreation was still there, and I could feel my heart hammering at the mere memories of my dad pushing me on the swings at the park.

I wish Jon had never said anything.

"Literally, we've been riding on this road our whol—" Jon kept going, but I was sick of talking about the past.

"Can we, like, not go down memory lane right now?"

Jon froze, his fingers gently curling around Liz's hand before he stopped talking, a frown fitting his lips. I felt a crush of guilt hit my chest at the sound of my words. But the way they were speaking about the town, it wasn't just the town, it was a mere reminder of everything I had done here. Like the bar at the edge of the street, where I got drunk off my ass one night and was found in the middle of the streets, passed out. Or the thrift store where Leslie, a girl in our freshman class, beat me up for a pair of 2-dollar sunglasses. My heart clenched.

"You just missed the street," Jon mumbled.

I looked to see Liz's fingers beginning to shake, her neck turning red and she grew nervous—I could tell.

"No, I didn't," she pushed.

"Yea, we needed to turn on Hertel, you just missed it."

She wasn't even turning her head to face Jon at the light, but I noticed the way it was tilted and almost as if she was in a daze. What the fuck?

"Liz," I started, when she suddenly snapped her head to look at the road, and I swallowed a lodge that had grown in my throat. Fuck.

"Here, here. The GPS says you can take a left on Murry and still make it before 10," Jon started, his fingers glossing across his phone, but his voice was shaky, like he was afraid to say what he wanted to say.

"I don't fucking care about the god damn party, Jon, I just want out of all of this. I just *want...* I jus—" She was rambling now, the car started to steer and I heard Jon gasp loudly and turn to grip the wheel, redness creeping up his fingertips.

He gripped her hand.

"Liz, breathe. You gotta breathe."

She sighed before turning and facing the window. In. Out. In. Out.

* * *

I didn't mean to, but somehow, I always made my way to the same place every Friday Night. A bar. A party. It wasn't that I enjoyed partying, I mean, how could I enjoy the sweaty people everywhere. Girls practically having sex with their boyfriends and the music that made me go deaf. It was the same music at each one of these parties. The same boring, pop music, and I was at the same fucking club each week.

I just wanted to leave my house. Distract myself for even an hour. I just hated being home. I hated being alone; *feeling* like I was alone. But once I realized I was found, I just wanted to be missing again.

Because I was my only constant, in the end, no one would be there for me—not my sister Elaine, or my other sister, or my mom, or my dad—they would never understand. Maybe *I* really didn't understand.

I brought a drink to my lips, swallowing down chunks as I breathed in, sitting on the stool. Some guy was strutting towards me, and in seconds, I was off my stool. He was bare-chested, jeans hanging low at his hips, and all I could think was that boys who try to show off their boxers are *disgusting.*

I could never date a guy who showed off his boxers thinking it made girls swoon. Some. Not me. But soon, that *was* me. I dated Flynn, totally taking out what I was thinking at this party, just throwing away everything I thought. Because with him, it never mattered. Nothing mattered.

He wound his fingers around my neck and I practically fell at the feel of his fingers on my skin. All I could think was how sweaty and big his hands were. And how I did not like his touch.

"Get off me!" I tried to push him off, and when he breathed, I smelt the vodka, and the way he slurred every syllable, the boy was drunk over his head. But wasn't I? I just stared at him, watching his tongue lap across his dry lips, and I shoved him off, watching his eyes lower to my breasts. I cringed. I stared down at my boobs, they hardly *were* boobs. God. I rolled my eyes, gripping his red hand and pushing it away from me.

"Trust me, if you think you're gonna have some hot and heavy sex tonight, you got the wrong girl."

"You hardly are one," he snickered, a lazy smile pulling at his lips, and I just stayed still. I didn't think his words would really hit me like it did, but for some reason, I pondered over it for so long. I looked down at my body, shaking my head like I was disappointed. Flynn fixed all of it. He made me feel different. Like someone I wasn't. Someone I maybe never wanted to be.

"Well, as far as I remember, I was born with a vagina, which you won't be seeing tonight." And then, I started walking out of the club and I could hear the boy running after me, but I ran as quick as I could in those damn heels. I know I was ditching Liz and Jon, but knowing them, they were probably upstairs somewhere doing God knows what. The heels were so tall! I almost tripped, but I pulled the door open and braced myself for the cold NYC wind.

It wasn't as cold as I thought that night, and for some reason, I always remembered the way the wind sifted through my hair that night; the smell of food carts filling my nose and the pop music playing from the bar I was just in. I grabbed my phone, thinking who could I call? Felicity was away, backpacking through whatever next country she chose to explore with her Fiancé, whom Mom and Dad met *once*. She probably didn't even have Wi-Fi connection or phone connection wherever she was. Can't call her. Could I call Elaine? I was positive Mom and Dad knew I was at a party, but they probably thought I was drunk. They always thought the worst of me. Not that they were really around to even see me.

I checked my wallet—maybe enough for a taxi.

But before I could phone an uber, out of literally nowhere, a boy stood beside me. Where the hell did he even come from? I remember I never really looked at him for a few seconds, I even stuffed my phone into my pocket, totally forgetting about the uber or about even getting home.

He was the first to talk.

"What's a girl like you doing in the city, outside of a club at like…" He paused, checking his watch. "2:12 a.m.?" I turned to face him, and without replying, I just looked at him, mapping the contours of his face to notice his eyes narrowing down at me. The corner of his lips tugged into a small smile and I knew my cheeks were heated. Everything felt heated. And all he was doing was looking at me. But I guess no one else ever did.

He raised an eyebrow, after I realized I was staring at him for way too long. I couldn't help myself, he was so messy looking that I just wanted to keep looking. He was this disastrous piece of art.

"Oh, I…" *What was I supposed to say?*

He looked confused, his eyes circling with something I couldn't figure out.

"Just out. With friends. At th… the…" I stammered, I was so nervous because I didn't want to screw it up before it even started. I didn't want to end it before it began.

"At the?"

I couldn't even speak; the words burned my tongue. I pointed at the club behind me.

"So, a party girl?" he had asked, his eyes pouring with glint. I remember taking offense to his comment; I wasn't really a party girl. I *went* to them. I drank like a fourth of a bottle. But I don't really *do* anything.

"No, not really. I just go to them. I really don't do anything." I managed to get out, and I realized how utterly stupid I sounded—I jus*t go* to them. What the hell does that even mean? Doesn't everyone just *go* to them?

He laughed, deep and breathless. I remember loving it. The way it sounded. But maybe that was because he was first to notice me, to see me, in a way no one else had. In a way I always wanted someone to see me.

It was so fucked up. But I was 17. I kissed one boy in my entire life, and seeing Felicity married, Elaine with her boyfriend, I wondered what it all felt like. The feeling of being wanted and loved and *needed.*

He glanced down at his waist, I realized they were hung low at his hips, and he pulled them up. It was as if he heard what I thought at the club. *Was he there?*

"Huh," was all he uttered. I stared down at my shoes. And that was when I smelt the vodka in his breath, and I stepped back a bit, a rush of cold air wrapping around my body. He smelt of smoke, lemon—but only VODKA filled my senses.

"Are you drunk?" I asked, my voice turning low.

"I'm 18. I can do what I want to. It's not like my... *my* anyone would care," he had said. 18? I guessed older. I noticed the dirt marks on the side of his nose and then he lifted his beanie off his head, running his hands through his hair and he sighed.

"That's not what I meant," he started with a long sigh. He sounded so annoyed with himself. Why did I care if he was drunk when it was clearly evident I was too? Where the fuck was my mind.

I laughed.

"It's all good. I don't know you." But the laugh came out choked, strangled even, and I turned away, unable to meet his eyes. I was afraid to look into them. Afraid of what I would have seen.

"I know you, though. Ria, right?" he had blurted, and I turned to look at him, my eyes growing a bit. *How, when, what*? I had never seen him. How could he even know me? I don't know myself.

"Huh," was all I said, acting as calm and cool as I could, but my heart was thundering in my chest, slipping out of its place.

He scratched his hand behind his neck and it was then when I realized how nervous he was too. And I was thankful that I wasn't the only one with a rapid heartbeat, and his cheeks were as red as mine; redness crawling up my arms and face and everywhere in between. I smiled at him. He kept looking at me, mapping the contours of my face, drinking in my sight. That made me nervous, self-conscious even—I never wanted him to stop looking at me the way he was—like I was some masterpiece. I wanted to ask him 'how' he knew me, if he had seen me, because NYC was a huge city. I would have remembered seeing him.

"See you. I…" He paused, breathing in. "Hope I see you again," he had told me with a smirk, before walking into the club I had just come out of. Just as I was about to ask him something—even though I didn't know what—Jon came rushing out of the door. His arms were wrapped around Elaine, and when she lifted her head, her eyes grew wide and she tried to scramble away from Jon, but he tightened his grip.

"What the fuck are you doing here, Elaine?"

She didn't respond, rather, averted her gaze from my face.

"She's drunk out of her head, Ria."

I moved closer to them.

"She's FIFTEEN!" I tried to grab Elaine's arm and it was only then when I realized how red her eyes were.

"And you're not my mom, Ria, st—" Elaine started, but her voice faltered away until she pressed her lips together and looked away again.

"What is actually happening to you?" Jon threw me a look that told me to stop pushing her, but all I could see was red, so I told Jon to find Liz in the club and I would figure out how to get Elaine home.

For a brief second, it looked like Elaine's face had fallen—like she realized something but it was gone in a second.

"I just wanted to go out," she said, slowly, like she was testing each word on her tongue before speaking.

"You *just* wanted to go out?"

"Like you said, escape is nice."

"It's *not* an escape, Elaine. You could go to jai—"

"I just want to run too…" she finally muttered, pushing her hands into her mom jeans.

"I want to see how it feels like to just forget, for even a bit. Like you do." And then it hit me, I turned around, because I knew my face had evaporated. I released a short breath. You don't ever forget. No matter how hard you try to forget about the problems, they just keep coming back.

I felt lonely. Going to these parties made me feel the same as everyone else, made me *feel* like I didn't have anything going on. But it was just a mere feeling.

"I'm wrong. I learned nothing from coming here. I escaped nothing from coming here."

"I just stalled it," I told her, and I took a bit to take in my own words.

"So? I want to stall."

"What fucking problems do you even have? You don't even know…" And instantly, I turned away and swallowed. Elaine raised her brows, pushing away from me. I realized right there, that you only know yourself. You don't know about anyone's problems but your own, and you can't act like you do. Because sometimes people will look at you with a smile on their face, when they're crying inside. You only know what goes on in your life, even if she was just my sister.

"It doesn't exist," I started, feeling an ache swim across my head. Everything was hurting.

"What the fuck?" Elaine started, confusion laced in her tone.

"Love. It just doesn't exist. Love doesn't give you a fucking forever. It stops. It falls apart…" I was rambling now, and I was about to spit out more shit before my eyes caught Jon and Liz stumbling out of the club.

"She's wasted." Jon said.

"Who isn't?" Elaine muttered back, and I swallowed a lump in my throat. Why was I always so emotional?

"Liz..." I started, walking towards her when she put her hand in front of her face.

"There was some duuuuudddeeeeee nammmmmeedddd something, I... I can't remember... he asked me if I needed a ride so we can... canannnnnnn go withhhhhh ciiimmmm," she drawled. Elaine was beginning to shut her eyes. And then, I turned around to see Liz stumbling to a car with the kid I met only 10 minutes ago.

"Him?" My hand flew to my mouth, and the guy simply grinned at me before curling his arm around Elaine's.

"Wait, wait hold up," I started, coughing and struggling to figure out how to phrase my words. I couldn't even find my words.

"We don't even know him. I mean..." I glanced at the guy. "You. You can't just take us home, I don't know you. We don't know you. It makes no sense to go home with a stranger, guys." I was on a fucking roll!

"The kid is being nice, Ria."

He turns around and looks at me in the eye, his lips curling into a hesitant smile. My vision was turning blurry and before I knew it, I could barely hold myself.

"Fine," I muttered, striding past Flynn and yanking his car door open.

"What's with the bit—" Elaine started, before turning out the window and puking all over the street curb.

"You're so fucking stupid, Elaine. Drunk, and you're like five," I said, my voice beginning to turn quiet.

"Fuck you. I can do what I want."

Flynn walked into the car, pulling at his front door.

"I'm sorry, I was just heading in the same direction so I thought, you know, kind deed." He turned back to look at me, and I just nodded.

"Why are you such a bitch?" Elaine started, her lips pressed into a thin line with frustration. I didn't want to start a fight. I was sick of them. Done arguing with everybody. Done trying to defend myself over everything. So, I remained quiet. It was almost like the silence was too loud.

Liz sat in the back seat, her arms wrapped around Jon's, who sat behind me. I noticed the back of Liz's neck shaking, and I was about to bring it up, let my drunk mind say the things I wouldn't say sober, but maybe it was just my bloodshot eyes fucking with my mind. And then again, I remained silent.

I hated the feeling. Flynn probably thought I was the biggest dick, and the worst part was, I didn't know why I was acting like this anyways. I wasn't normally so mad. All I could see was red, and no matter what anyone said, my heart just flopped out of my chest.

"She's the biggest fuc—" Elaine muttered a string of words, Flynn turned back and I kept my face hidden. Elaine angrily crossed her arms across her chest as I watched her fingers graze the charm bracelet Dad gave her. I rolled my eyes.

I gave Flynn the directions and it was the only words I said through the whole car ride. He kept glancing back and behind me, Liz kept snickering. I kept telling myself it was just the alcohol getting to her. But it looked like Flynn wasn't even trying to hide it. His cheeks never turned red as so many do when they're caught looking, but he just raised his eyebrow and I shrugged my shoulders, still not uttering a word.

Jon asked Flynn if he could work the radio.

"Oh yea, man, course. Here, choose the station. My phone's plugged in though, so I apologize…" He looked at me again. Jon smiled. "If the music's bad, don't judge."

"Switch it to some camp rock baby, pleeeaassseeeee," Liz slurred and Jon stuck his middle finger up.

"Fuck no, that's some shit."

Flynn shrugged.

"I JUST WANNA PLAY MY MUSIC," he started singing, and this cracked me and Liz up. But we were so out of it, anything was making me laugh. That's just what I kept telling myself.

"What school do you all go to?" Flynn asked, a smile in his voice. And this made me smile. And then I was just smiling all over, my nose, my eyes, my face, everything. Because this kid couldn't stop looking at me. And I couldn't stop paying attention to it. And with one mere look, I could already feel my entire face burning.

Fuck. Fuck. WHAT THE FUCK.

I turned away, but this made his lips curl into a small smirk. I wanted to jump out of the window.

"Uhhh, how about you stop us here?" I started, swallowing. What was I doing?

Liz turned back, raised her brows.

"We're like 4 miles from home, still. The fuck, Ria, you can't even stand right now, let alone walk," Jon said.

"Exceri..." I slurred. "Size," I finished, the word making me giggle. Everything felt so funny and the world felt light, like it was spinning on the wrong axis.

"I mean, if the lady wants to be dropped off here she ca—" Flynn started, and I found myself eagerly nodding my head.

Jon put his hand on Flynn's shoulder.

"She would get lost the second we left her on the curb."

"Shut up," I muttered.

Flynn laughed, but it wasn't a typical laugh—it was low, and deep, and his eyes twinkled, and it made me feel like *my* eyes were twinkling, and it made me feel giddy and jumpy. I couldn't tell whether I hated or loved it. *Fuck.*

"Here's your house," Flynn finally said, and at first, I thought it was mine and Elaine's stop, and I was already unbuckling my seat belt, ready to exit, when Flynn turned to me and winked.

He WINKED.

"Not your stop yet. Just chill. Breathe and chill."

"You're telli—" I started, and then pressed my lips into a line. I gotta keep my mouth shut or God knows what shit I would spit out. At the time, I never understood the importance of the first words people utter to you. Or the first time you meet them. I just never cared too much of it. But in those few seconds, his body was still and unmoving on the ground, I just remembered this day. It was as if, for so long, I just wanted to forget it. But it seemed the things I tried my hardest to forget, seemed to be the only thing I could ever remember. And then, he told me I looked cute, and I couldn't get over it. The words weren't even that big of a deal. I just remember loving it.

You're cute.

"You're cuter," I had said, stuttering and my eyes growing. You're CUTE? CUTE? *God, what is wrong with me.*

"I mean hot or handsome or wh—"

He laughed again. That deep, low laugh that made my heart drum across my chest.

"Hot and handsome, both suffice. Cute's my favorite though." His lips lifted into a smirk, and in only a few seconds, that smirk turned into a smile, a short, gentle one that spread across his face. He seemed so happy, and it was then when I knew, this was the Flynn I liked. Thought so at least. Not the stranger whose heart had almost stopped beating. Not the stranger who tried to burn himself to death and overdose on hard drugs. He was someone else. He was unrecognizable. He was Flynn. But not *my* Flynn.

And out came more words.

"What's your number?" I asked, and he practically stopped the car. I didn't pay attention to it before, but the way his entire face almost evaporated in a way, and the way he slowed down the car, like he had to try to think of the few numbers.

"Really?" he had asked me so quietly, and I wondered, why? We were alone in a car. It was my turn to laugh.

"*Really*," I mumbled almost breathlessly, because he had leaned closer—his face only mere inches from mine. Too close. And then for a few seconds, he didn't respond. He just stared at me, mapping the contours of my face, and I all I could think was *fuck acne, fuck my face.*

"Your freckles are cute," he finally murmured softly, before backing away and actually telling me his number. My phone had slipped from my fingers so I bent down to grab it, but he did it before me, smiling and handing it to me.

"Yea, you're gonna need this, especially now that you got me to text."

I rolled my eyes.

"Who said I would reply?"

He stared at me. Long and hard.

"The fact you asked for it…" He laughed and simply shook his head, gripping the car mirror.

Fuck me.

No actually, please don't.

Fuck. Fuck.

"Here's your stop," he said, a smile in his voice. But I was completely out of it, and for some reason, I was angry with myself. I couldn't pinpoint why, but I could feel that I was.

"Uh," I started as I gripped Elaine's arm, yanking her out of the car. What was I trying to say?

"Oh, right. Thanks so much for the ride. See you around, I guess."

"I guess I will call you," Flynn said, and I merely nodded my head, brought my hand up to wave as I half walked, half ran to the front door. Elaine was already inside, but her face had collapsed.

I yanked the front door open and could hear Dad's yelling from the first floor. He was on the third. I laced my fingers with Elaine's, pulling her towards me. She snaked her arms around my neck and it was then when I realized her body was shaking with tears. But I just stood there, not knowing how to react. Elaine wasn't crying because Dad and Mom were arguing. She was crying because she knew it wasn't going to stop and because they're never not yelling.

"It's never over. You tell me every single t—" Elaine started, slowly pulling away from me.

"Hey, I don't know everything."

"Or anything," Elaine muttered.

"Just go sleep," I mumbled, pointing up the stairs just as the sound of a coffee cup fell to the hard wood and cracked.

Elaine rapidly turned to face me, her fingers trembling.

"I can't sleep, not like this."

"I won't fucking sleep on the floor," Mom yelled, I could almost hear her throwing pillows around. I turned to look at Elaine, who pressed her fingers into her ears and pierced her eyes shut, praying that this was all just a dream of pointless words and lies.

Dad didn't utter a word for a bit. I could feel footsteps moving towards Mom; I hoped Mom wasn't pushing away. I heard the sound of faint sobbing and I could picture it already:

Mom stuffing her face into her hands as tears shook her entire body. She would start screaming. She always did when she cried. It was her thing. She went mad. They both did.

Dad would grip her shoulders, try to soothe her, but it wouldn't work, resulting in Dad almost always using the guestroom and Mom taking their bedroom.

"Of course, you're not sleeping on the floor. You get the bed, I can take the floor," Dad muttered frantically.

Mom let out a deep breath. She couldn't control her sobs.

"I just want…" she paused, her voice soft and too quiet for me to understand what she was saying. I stayed near the door but couldn't make out the rest of their words. It's like they always try to act like their fights don't exist. That somehow, me and Elaine are just deaf and can't hear a word or scream or cry that comes out of that damn room.

Well, Mom, I guess you just forget we live here altogether.

I sighed.

"Just think of it as a nightmare, it's going to stop by morning," I said in a low voice, realizing how faint my voice sounded.

"What's going to stop?" Elaine started breathlessly. "Them yelling? You and I both know it's more than yelling. The drinking? Watch Dad get some woman pregnant? Watch Mom leave? Or watch Dad just run away in the middle of the…"

"Stop doing this to yourself. You're making crazy shit up. They're parents, a couple, and couples argue all the time. It's just part of it," I told her as I slipped my flats off. Those words were in a constant repeat in my head, I had it all planned out, every sentence, every response. Because I don't really know what will happen. I can't say everything is going to be alright. Because it might not be.

"A part of marriage is going out, getting drunk at 3:15, coming home and hitting your wife with a beer bottle?"

I pressed my lips into a thin line.

"Just go sleep," I finally muttered quietly, as I started making my way towards the stairs.

"I fucking told you, I can't," Elaine repeated.

"Then take a shower. Just distract yourself."

She glanced up the stairs and, for a few seconds, we drowned in tranquility.

"Why do you always try to act like it doesn't happen?"

I sighed.

She kept going.

"Why do you just keep lying to yourself, Ria? Yea, fights are normal. But *their* fights aren't." And then she slipped out the door, disappearing like she always did.

Chapter Two

"You probably won't get the internship," Elaine teased me as she grabbed the box of Cheerios from the cabinet.

Mom said nothing. She didn't even know I applied for it. It was 6 months ago and I thought it would be interesting to work for a car company, so I applied for the fun of it. Funny, because I never ended up working there anyways. I turned to look at Mom as she buttoned her work shirt on, but she didn't even look me in the eye. I noticed how bloodshot her eyes were, and they weren't from crying.

"Thanks for the support," I mumbled as I hastily poured milk into the bowl.

"Is it even paid?"

"Most aren't," Mom finally uttered and I didn't even bother to turn around.

"And she talks!" Elaine muttered, and I snickered. But as I saw Mom's face, I turned around.

"Not the best idea to get drunk on a night you have work, is it now?" I said, and even I knew it was a low blow, but I wanted so bad for her to hear it from me.

"I'm n—" she coughed. "Drunk." Her voice turned into a mere whisper, and she quickly turned her face and attempted to block it with her sleeve.

"Hungover?" Elaine offered.

"How was the waiter?" I muttered, packing my bags.

"Waiter?" She was so bad at hiding her emotions.

"What was his name again? James... no, wait, Declan? Or wait, that was the *other one.*"

Mom never replied and I knew I hit her tough spot. I wish Dad was here. I wish someone was here to pick up on it. Instead, she grabbed her cup of coffee and staggered towards the garage door without a sound.

* * *

After stealing 10 bucks from Mom's bag, I ran out the door just because I didn't want to see Mom's face. I knew she was crying, I could hear it as I pulled the front door open. But I didn't spare a glance. And I remember hating myself for it. I just kept walking down the sidewalk, like my body was moving before my mind was. It was processing everything after I was doing it.

I called Liz.

"Hey hey, you here?"

I could hear Jon in the background. Jon and Liz were that on-and-off-again couple, but had been dating since 8th grade. They already had baby names prepared and I already called flower girl at their wedding.

"I see youuu!" Liz screeched, and I wiped at my eyes before turning around as Liz's car rolled onto my driveway. As Liz rolled the window down, her eyes raked my face and she lifted her finger out and gently touched my eyes.

"Were you crying?" she asked me, and I quickly wiped at my eyes again. *No! I wasn't crying! Droplets of rain were just rolling on my cheeks!*

"No no, when I washed my face the water just got in my eye." *Water just got in my eye.* Jon wrapped his arm around

Liz's waist and I turned to get into the backseat. I didn't realize he was coming with us every morning, and I watched his hands slip into hers. Liz's face lit up and I realized, just one touch, one glance from Jon could completely change her mood.

"SAT scores come out today," Jon said, and he turned his head, throwing me a smile. I nodded my head, the smallest smile fitting my lips.

"I fucking bombed that. That stupid test we took for like 4 hours?" Liz muttered, and I laughed. Just to act fine. Just so they wouldn't be able to tell the difference.

"You probably got a 1600, Jon," I said with a smile, and he turned red, scratching his neck.

"Your voice—Ria, you're a terrible liar," Jon said, shaking his head.

"Liar?" I repeated.

"You're upset," he said.

"So? People cry sometimes. Crying helps," I muttered, turning so he wouldn't be able to see me.

"You don't need to wipe the tears away, it's just us," Liz said.

"It makes me feel like, like I'm weak," I muttered breathlessly.

"You're not pathetic if you cry, Ria. It just shows that whatever happened, you care a lot for it."

"But what if you're crying because you don't care?" I uttered quietly, wiping at my eyes. I'm upset because I didn't go back and soothe Mom. She's my mom. *Mom. Mom.* Such a weird word. A mom is someone who should be there for you, take care of you, love you. Ask you how your day's been. If you have a boyfriend. Or if you failed your test. She *should care.*

"You care more then you realize it," Liz told me with a sad smile, and I merely glanced out the window.

"What even happened?"

"I'm a fuck up," I just repeated, pressing my cheek to the window.

"We all are, Ria. We all have screw ups, we all do wrong shit, and you gotta accept that it isn't just you that feels that way. We're all human."

I changed the subject.

"How do you think you did on the SAT?"

Jon just stared at me, narrowing his eyes at my face and I just stared back, hoping he would just reply.

"Community college, here I come," he said, and I shook my head.

"You're not allowed to say that, you're literally going to go to Yal—"

He cut me off, "*Stanford.*"

"Same thing!"

"No, actually, one is called YALE and the other i—"

"Okay please, you know that thing where words come out of your mouth?" I started, my lips curling into a small smirk.

"Talking?" He quickly bent down and placed a chaste kiss on Liz's cheek, and for a second, I was about to stop speaking. I don't get why it always affects me so much.

"Yea, stop that. Thanks!"

* * *

Signs for HARSHENS SCHOOL HOMECOMING were everywhere and ballots to vote for queen and king were scattered across the hallway. I turned to see Elaine running down the halls, carrying a white poster and holding her favorite candy, Hershey's on a bag and her entire face red and lit with smiles.

"Brian, he just asked me to homecoming!" she said breathlessly, and for a second, I just stared at her, before senses kicked in and I gave her a hug.

"Why is it a big deal? He is your *boyfriend*?" Boyfriend. Boyfriend. The word felt so funny. Sometimes I just wonder how it all works, how it even happens. It's so hard to like someone and have that person like you back, but the way Elaine talks about it, like it's the easiest and simplest thing in the world.

"I know, I know. But I didn't think he was gonna formally ask me, and he did, and oh my God, it was so cute. In front of so many people too. He looked so nervous to—" I couldn't hear any more, but I made sure my lips pulled into a smile.

"Yea, awwww, that's great! I have a test retake, so see you lat—" She cut me off this time.

"I won't be home tonight, going on a double date with Gerry and Fiona."

"Just text me," I told her, slipping down the halls into the math classroom. I needed this teacher to write up a recommendation for me, so I was his teacher's assistant and helped him grade tests. Everyone was being asked to the dance and I was more sad than happy, and I hated how I was feeling both of those at the same time. I didn't understand how I could be happy and sad and angry all in the same second. I loved seeing Elaine's face break into smiles. I have this theory that everyone looks 10 times prettier when they smile. She doesn't do it enough. I love seeing Liz laugh and giggle every time Jon spares her one glance, he looks at her the same way he did three years ago, and as if she's the only person in the room.

But sometimes, I wish that it was me too, that could feel all that.

"That was so nerve wrecking!" Brian said as he passed by me and I laughed, shaking my head.

"She was going to say yes," I told him, rolling my eyes.

"I know, I know. But she's not a dance person so I was worried."

"That is true, she hates those type of things—the ones that every couples do."

Brian glanced at the wall, his lips curling into a brief smile and then shrugged.

"Yea, it's why I love her. Don't tell her any of this…" He started, his voice turned quiet. "But my last relationship was so boring, plain. She wanted to go the movies, she wanted to do double dates, go prom shopping, but Elaine's different. She stood out. She makes love feel different, not fake, not a lie—she makes it *real*." And for a couple seconds, Brian just stopped speaking, like he was taking in his words after he said them. And I dwelled on it for a bit before laughing, and pulling him into a hug.

"I gotta go grade some tests, have fun on your date!" I told Brian and he turned red, bringing the palm of his hand to the back of his neck before waving at me and rushing to get to lunch.

I ran into the math classroom and put my bag to the ground.

"Hi, Mr. Gonzales, sorry I was late," I mumbled, mentally shaking my head at myself before planting myself onto the stool beside his desk.

"It's fine, it's fine. The pre-calc students turned in the homework today, so just go through it. Make sure they did all the correct problems, and showed work, and then put a star at the top. I'm going to go get some lunch," he tells me, and I nod my head as my fingers snake around the paper and grab a pen. I hastily go through the papers but, for some reason, I can't focus, and I feel sad all over again. Why do I let these small things affect me so much? It's like the small things are more important and more impactful than things that should actually affect me. Maybe that's just how life works.

I draw stars on the papers and finally put them in one large pile before the bell rings. I write Mr. Gonzales a small note, grab my bag and meet up with Liz who's typing away on her phone beside the door.

"There you are," I tease, shutting the classroom door. She doesn't immediately respond, so I snap my hands in front of her.

"LIZZZZZZZ."

"Ohhh sorry, Ria. I was texting Amy about prom shopping plans. You wanna come?"

"Why the fuck would you go with Amy? She's a little snake that spread that rumor you got pregnant, like, freshman year."

"People change," she muttered, her fingers clicking away at her phone.

"She literally told like half the school you had se—" I started, completely confused.

"Two chances. People get two chances."

"It's been more than two, Liz. One mistake is okay, two chances is the limit, but by three, you should know then it's done and she's just using you for something." The way the words clicked off my tongue almost made me sound jealous of a friendship that basically didn't exist, but I didn't want to come off that way.

"So?"

"There's only so much faith you can have in people." I don't know what I was saying really, I was just blurting things out.

"Chill, Ria?"

"Do what you want, I can't go anyway, because you know…" Suddenly, my voice lowered. I yanked at my backpack strap.

"No date, no dress." Why the fuck was I making such a big deal out of this? It was nothing. It was just a dance.

But then, the other part of me wondered that there was a reason people freaked out so much over prom and dances. Like, you go buy a beautiful, expensive dress to wear it once, for maybe three hours, then you never touch it anyway and prom becomes a memory, just like all others. I never even bothered going. But for some reason, this year felt different. I *wanted* to go. Seeing everyone else get asked—including my younger sister—I just felt a twinge of something, a need to want to be asked and to go with someone who would want to ask me. And I did want someone to snake their arms around my waist, pull me close, and dance to one of the trashy songs they always play at high school dances.

I laughed at myself.

One more year and I'm out of this hell-hole. Plus, I didn't have a thing for any high school guys. Not that it would really matter. No one wanted me like that. Until I met *him*. I refrain from even saying his name; I don't want to remember all the times it slipped off my lips. It used to be the easiest word to say, something that used to be said so quickly and so effortlessly. That all felt like so long ago. I just hoped if I kept thinking of it as something that was a mere dream, something where I truly wasn't present, then maybe I could slowly forget it even happened. That he even existed.

That *us* never existed. But I couldn't, because he was everywhere I turned. And I hated myself even more for it, for letting him affect me so much, for letting him come into my life and changing every little thing about it. Because I let him, and I had no one to blame but me for the whole thing.

So it's a thing now.

I didn't know how else to describe it, or him.

Because you never even knew him.

I don't think you ever know all of someone. Everyone is unpredictable. And people are never as they seem, even if they look at you with a smile, they might be frowning inside, or if they tell you they love you, when they don't know what love is.

"You could still come you know. I would love a friend's advice on the dress," Liz said, breaking me from my thoughts.

I rolled my eyes.

"Go have fun with Amy," I mumbled.

Liz finally pushed her phone into her pocket.

"Okay look, the only reason I'm going with her, is she said she would pay for my dress if she had someone to go shopping with. Imma use that to my advantage, of course. But please, don't leave me with that brat for four hours!"

"She's going to pay FOR YOUR DRESS? Hold up."

"Her dad's, like, loaded; gave her a ridiculous amount of money. And she said, whatever she had left over, she would pay for me. And all I have to do is act like her friend and go shopping with her."

"Why? Like, why does she even need a friend to go shopping?"

"Look, not everyone is like you and prefers to shop alone like a looooooooseeeerrrrr."

I faked a gasp.

"Hey hey, I like going on alone because I don't like my friends clothing styles and opinions meshing with whatever I wanna buy."

Liz rolled her eyes, but a smile made its way to her lips.

"Amy's complicated," Liz finally sighed. I shrugged.

"Isn't everyone?"

"But she's like different complicated. She's like that white top that might look good in light blue jeans but doesn't look good in *dark blue* jeans."

"What the fuck does that even mean?"

"I just don't want her to get pissed off. You know what she did last time."

I lowered my voice, a soft smile making its way to my lips.

"You can't ever, ever let someone control you so much you're afraid to say what you really wanna say or what you really wanna do. People like that can fuck you up, Liz. And you're already letting her affect you."

Liz released a breath.

"I can't let her do what she did last time. I mean, Jon didn't talk to me for so long because he thought I cheated on him, Ria!"

I shook my head.

"You knew the truth. You knew. It didn't matter what she said—" Liz cut me off, her face turning white, and that's when I realized this was a lot more than what she was giving me.

"But it did. She almost screwed up me and Jon. I just need to go, be on her good side for a bit."

I just stared at her for a couple seconds, afraid to say anything.

"Okay. Okay." I gripped her shoulders and pulled her into a quick hug.

"See youuuuuuuuuuu."
"Love you, Ree."

Chapter Three
Three Hours Later

I came home scared. But then I realized, Dad was away at work and Mom was wherever she was; that I could finally breathe.

Breathe.

Was that bad? How I felt so good without them home. I shook my head and hastily yanked out of my phone to see, like, 8 texts from Liz.

BABE: HELP HELP

BABE: oh my God the shit this girl says i cant

BABE: omg she picked up this yellow dress and i wanna tell her it looks so ugly on her but u taught me to be a kind-ish human

BABE: okay thx for the responses

BABE: love ya too!!!

BABE: oh fuck she just told me who she likes lol I'm dead g2g

I called her.

Liz immediately picked up, her breath fanning across the phone.

"She's changing in the dressing room right now. Can't talk. But you know who you should talk to? That kid, Flynn." I could almost feel Liz's wink from across the phone. And the worst part was how heated my entire body felt, just at the mere mention of his name. And I realized how completely stupid I was for getting so nervous over someone I didn't even know.

But now I know I never actually knew him. I just kept telling myself I did because I was his girlfriend, and I thought girlfriends should know all these things about their boyfriends. But I knew nothing, I just acted like I did.

Fuck.

I thought I could have moved on from the whole thing. But I guess some people just can't move on. For some, they're always going to remember the little parts of a relationship, a friendship that they can't ever forget. And they can't always put on a face to last. Some of these things stick with us for years, for forever. The little pieces and parts we think we can stitch back to cover up the remains and reminders, aren't strong enough.

"Ria…" Elaine stepped into the hall, her arms merged with Brian's, and I laughed.

"I thought you were going shopping?" I raised my eyebrow, wanting to laugh at the way the redness painted across her cheeks.

"She did do some shopping. And *buying.*" Brian winked, and I faked a gag. Elaine pulled at his shoulder muttering a series of words like "Shut up, you dick."

I caught the way he raised a brow at dick.

"God, you two are just…" I started with a laugh.

"Adorable? Thanks!"

I rolled my eyes as Elaine gripped Brian's arm tighter.

I hadn't ever seen her so happy.

"We're going out to dinner, PF Chang's," Brian told me, pushing his Converse onto his feet.

As Elaine passed me, carefully brushing her shoulder against mine, she whispered, "Call him back." I turned to look at her, attempting to act confused, but she wasn't buying it.

And with that, the door slammed shut, leaving me alone. And this was the first time in so long where I absolutely hated it.

* * *

"Hey, uh... hi, Flynn. It's Ri... Henrietta." I swallowed, fuck, what the fuck am I doing? I pressed the palm of my hand gently to my skirt, noticing the redness crawl up my fingertips. He breathed into the phone but didn't say anything for a couple seconds.

"I remember you," he finally murmured, his voice quiet and I swallowed again.

"Yea, so I was wondering if you wanted to... maybe see a movie or hang out or—"

"How about you come over to my place?"

I thought for a second.

"Why not just dinner?" I mumbled, embarrassed.

"At my place?" he said, firmly, and before I could even argue, he muttered a soft goodbye, and ended the call. Before I could even argue with myself, or maybe figure out what just happened, I gripped my phone, and hastily started texting him.

"Please," he breathed, "it would be... fun."

ME: Whats ur adress?

FLYNN: I knew you would come around ;)

I didn't respond to that.

FLYNN: 705 NW HERTEL STRET

ME: See you then.

FLYNN: Looking forward to it.

I pressed the off button on my phone, throwing it into my bed and hugging myself. What did I just agree to? I couldn't even tell. I didn't even know the guy and I just agreed to having dinner at his house. I mean, where else do thinks start? Right? We have to start somewhere. There's gotta be that beginning, and I guess, this just happens to be mine.

Or *ours.*

Elaine walked into the room, and I turned quickly to my dresser mirror to make sure my entire face wasn't still completely drowning in redness. I cleared my throat, watching the way my fingers made their way towards each other and Elaine's smirk grew across her face.

"Flynn?"

"NO, it was my husband." I rolled my eyes, lacing my fingers on the pink straps of my purse and yanking it across my shoulder.

"Why do you always, always, always have to sound like the biggest bitch?" Elaine's eyes bored into mine and I stepped back. My chest fell.

"What do you me—"

Elaine took in a deep breath before opening her mouth again.

"I hope he changes you, maybe makes you smile more and frown a little bit less. Maybe laugh more so your face glows up. I hope he makes things better for you because, God knows, you need it." Her lips curved upwards into a sad smile before she snapped her arm about my knob, slowly pulling the door open and stepping out into the hall. I heard her release a series of breaths, almost like she was trying to stop herself from crying.

It was like words burned my tongue, so nothing came out. Even when I did hear her sniffing, I still didn't leave or utter a word. Maybe that was my problem.

"Elaine?" I called out softly, hoping the cries wouldn't block my voice. When she stopped sniffling, I knew she heard me but she never did reply.

"Dad's home," was all she mumbled, and I stood up, immediately dropping my purse and rushing down the stairs. Dad's home? I remember when I was 9, coming home to Mom who was always cooking fried eggs, Dad sitting on the counter with his head stuffed in a magazine, stealing as many kisses and glances he could from Mom. Mom would giggle like it was the first time she ever saw him. I haven't heard Mom laugh in a long time. Not a true one. Not the way she used to. Sometimes, I don't think they realize that I notice these things that Elaine notices.

I peered down the hall to see Dad frantically talking to someone on the phone—sounded like someone he knew well—but I must have made some sound or breath, because his voice turned quiet and he put the phone on the counter. He glanced up.

I turned away, pressing myself against the wall.

It's reached a point where I'm scared to speak to *my dad*. The same man who came to my musical performances and the same man who came to every one of my soccer matches.

Fuck this. I turned down the hall and plastered the fakest smile I could.

"Ri—" Henrietta." I corrected, watching my distance.

Dad did not respond. Instead, he gripped his cell phone and pressed something. I guess he was ending the call. My eyes wouldn't leave the phone that was on the counter and Dad noticed it.

"It was pizza," he muttered, slipping his bag off his shoulder and putting it on the couch.

"Pizza? Mom's cooking pasta tonight though," I told him, just as my voice was slowly turning quiet, like I was about to cry.

"Do you see her? She's not home. Work probably caught her up."

Work.

Work.

WORK.

"Was it really pizza, Dad? Don't lie to me. You got all quiet when I came down the stairs. Just tell me who it was, what her name is, because I won—"

Dad's face fell.

"*Her?*" He turned away from me, his voice drifting into a mere whisper. I knew I hit something.

"Yea, who is it this time?" I asked, my voice barely audible. I glanced at the tile floor, unable to meet his eyes, afraid of what I would see.

"Why do you always… always expect me to cheat on your Mom? I'm still here, trying to make this god damn marriage work for you two—" I cut him off.

"For me and Elaine? Don't make us the reason you're staying with Mom. You stay with her because you love her. You stay with her because you want her. You don't stay with her for us, I don't want that. She won't want that," I muttered breathlessly like I was tired. But I was just worried of the way the words would string together, if they even made any sense.

"You just don't get it, you won't ever until you're married with two kids," he muttered, turning towards the fridge.

"Then explain it to me, help me get it. Because right now, all I see is a man who has no care in the world left for the so-called love of his life," I mumbled, the words slipping off my tongue before I thought them through. I just wanted to know. It didn't make sense. I don't want my dad to stay married to someone he doesn't love, even when we know mother is surely cheating on him. But it's like he doesn't care about that. Like he doesn't care Mom could be lying in someone else's bed, kissing someone else's lips. Like he expects it.

For a couple seconds, we drowned in complete tranquility. And then, his lips carved a sad, short smile.

"Ever wonder how love feels like, Henrietta? But it's different when you're 40 and married. Even when that love begins to fall apart, you stay with them because of every little thing you've been through. You don't just throw away 20 years of marriage. Not like that, not when you have two kids. Just..." He paused.

"Think about that," Dad uttered faintly, before leaving the kitchen without another glance.

Chapter Four

"This dress or this one?" Liz held up two white dresses, and was it bad that at the sheer site of the dresses, I was already annoyed?

I quickly looked at both of them, unable to tell the difference.

"This one." I pointed at the one with the ruffles and Liz shook her head, gently putting the dress down.

"I like the other one, fits me better I think."

I threw my hands in the air.

"Why ask me then?"

Liz rolled her head back and chuckled, slowly shaking her head back and forth.

"Ria, breathe, breathe. Chill. Breathe. Chill. I know your date with Flynn has gotten you all wack—"

I put my finger in the air, my smile growing into a laugh.

"If you say one more word about—"

"Date! Date! Date! Date!"

I rolled my eyes, unable to stop the laughs that escaped my lips.

"I'm still worried. I mean, going to his house, already? He just seemed so… persistent."

Liz shrugged, her fingers latched around the hem of her dress as she yanked the dress tag off.

"It's not like he's going to have sex with you. Maybe he wanted it more formal. I mean, I'm not even gonna try to understand the male mind, but don't stress so much about the location, Ria. Also, persistency is so cute. It's like him showing you how much he wants you."

"Oh my God, you're honestly the stupidest human I've met."

I flipped Liz off.

"It's just dinner, not really a big deal," I told her, despite my entire body heating up. Why the fuck was I so nervous? People went on dates all the time. But first dates, maybe I could make it a big deal in my head. I just didn't understand how this all worked.

"At his house," Liz murmured, raking through the fridge with a satisfied expression, when she lifted out the new bottle of strawberry lemonade, twisting the cap off.

"Dinner. At his house," I added.

"At his house, *alone*," Liz continued, her lips slowly curling upwards into a smirk just as I threw one of her dresses at her face. Just as I was about to mutter some shit about her and Jon, someone started to knock on the front door. I walked down the hall, peeking through the curtains to see Jon.

"Yo! Jon's here!" I yelled down the hall as I wrapped my hand around the knob and pulled it open revealing Jon with rose flowers. It looked like his entire face was smiling, his nose, his eyes, his face.

"Shit, hide the dresses," Liz muttered just as Jon stepped inside, slipping his sneakers off.

"So, I got her some flowers, I don't even know why, but I was there and you k—" I released a string of laughs at how nervous he looked, like it was the first time they were going out.

"Kitchen." I pointed with the smallest smirk painting my lips just as my phone rang.

"Guess who's calling?" Liz yelled from the other side of the room, and in seconds, I ran to the living room, gripped my phone as tightly as I could and eagerly picked up the call. God, why was I turning into such a sap.

And then, before I could even place my phone on my ear, the front door opened and my mom stepped inside—more like stumbled. She couldn't even look me in the eye, and it was then when I saw the tears tickling her cheeks.

"Li—" I started softly, but she already got it and exited with Jon through the back door.

"Mom," I said, my voice barely audible as she shakily slipped her shoes off. Before I could say anything, she ran into the bathroom and slammed the door, twisted it, and locked it. It was then when I heard her—puking?

My feet moved before my head, and I stood beside the door, my hands covering the knob.

"Mom?" I whispered against the wood, and I could hear her stand up. She opened the door, attempting to cover her mouth, but I pushed her fingers away.

"What was that?"

She merely glanced back at the toilet.

She shrugged.

"Dinner gone wrong."

The worst part was I couldn't really argue with that. I couldn't be, like, "that didn't sound like dinner going wrong." Because maybe it was. But before I could ask her anything else, she disappeared up the stairs, leaving me to drown in my endless thoughts.

She didn't come down for dinner. And that night, Dad didn't come home till late. It was just me and Elaine, but Elaine wasn't eating, merely twisting her fork into her food, occasionally biting down on salad.

"What's going on?" I finally asked her, her eyes on the food.

"Nothing," she mumbled, averting her gaze from my face.

Before I could respond, she pressed the fork into her green salad.

"Everything. What the hell is happening to my mom? She's been sleeping since, like, 4."

I shrugged.

"Late hours at the hospital. Her late night work shifts affect the sleeping schedule," I muttered as I cleaned the dish and looked back at Elaine's expression. She didn't utter a word—barely nodding her head like she didn't necessarily agree with me but had something else in mind.

"Nothing's going on," I finished, noticing the way my voice was turning quiet and growing thin. Fuck. I turned to see Elaine staring at me, her eyes growing before she shook her head and walked out of the kitchen without a word.

"Nothing always means something. Nothing just doesn't exist. There's always something," Elaine murmured, trailing away in thought.

"I've learned it with Brian and watching Dad. People just use that word as an excuse, and I hate it. Mom will come downstairs, act like nothing just happene—" I cut her off, afraid she was going to think so darkly, and maybe it was true, but for now, I just didn't want to think like that.

"She could just be sick, you know. It doesn't have to be so complicated."

"With Mom, nothing's ever simple, Ria. You know that." Elaine turned away, her voice drifting away into a whisper before snaking her hand around her bag and walking towards the door.

"Uh, where are you going?" I yelled but she didn't even bother responding with words, the sound of the door slamming shut being my response. I released a breath I never realized I was holding before putting the dishcloth away.

Mom still hadn't come down, so I left leftovers if she ever would. I called Dad. But it went straight to voicemail.

12:07 a.m – no answer.
12:30 a.m – no answer.
1:35 a.m. – no answer.
1:42 a.m. – voicemail.

My hands practically scrambled to reach my phone from my bedside table, and I quickly pressed it. For a couple seconds, I couldn't hear anything but just, maybe, breaths. And then I heard the faint sound of someone talking, a woman who sounded exactly like Liz. "Put it away," she muttered, but the sound was so distant I couldn't make out anything other than the sound of it being a woman, and then the voicemail abruptly ended.

Chapter Five

Dad didn't come home that Saturday morning. I spent the majority of breakfast studying for my Spanish oral for Monday. And by one, was dead exhausted and called Liz to see if she wanted to head out for lunch. But before I even bothered grabbing my phone, I realized tonight was the night of the school dance and she was probably out getting her hair and her makeup done.

I glanced at my phone, seeing Flynn's two missed calls. His mere name on the screen made my chest rise up and down. Was this supposed to happen? Was I supposed to feel like this so quickly? And then my voice buzzed with a text.

Flynn: Answer my call.

I didn't respond for a bit, thinking of how to respond to it. I was putting in way too much thought into this. He sounded so persistent. I didn't know if I liked it or was scared of it.

Me: Whats it about? I'm out.

Flynn: No you're not :)

What the fuck?

He called again, I didn't answer. I was too much of a nervous mess when he called.

Flynn: Pick up, Henrietta. You might like the call.

Me: What's that mean?

Flynn: Pick up to find out.

He called again, I sucked in a harsh breath and pressed 'answer' before putting the phone on speaker.

"Hey," he said through the line, his voice strangely quiet.

"Hi," I mumbled, my voice was so soft and so inaudible, I didn't think he even heard a bit, but the second he laughed, that fucking laugh, I knew he did.

"You gotta learn to not be nervous. I don't know how I will ever be able to kiss you if your heart's gonna flip-flop at a mere call." I swallowed, feeling heat run through my cheeks. No one's ever said that. No one's ever said it, *like that.*

He laughed into the line.

"Henrietta, I was kidding," he mumbled.

I didn't reply, instead, bit my lip.

"Okay, actually, I wasn't kidding at all. But, I just met you and…" he started, his words, slow. And it was like he was thinking his way through every little thing he said.

"I get it." *I didn't.*

"I don't want to come off weird."

"You're not." *Yes, you are.*

"You sure?" *No, I'm not.*

"I don't like people who lie," he muttered.

"And you're saying I am?"

"No, I'm just telling you ahead of time," he said.

"Well, who does like people lying?"

"Look, I don't know… just… people always hide what they actually feel. Even when it's pointless. Like they say what they want the other person to hear, you know?"

"You're getting so deep over something so small," I said, chuckling into the line.

He sighed, almost like he was annoyed. I imagined his hands running through his hair.

"I just don't want th—" he started, his voice carrying off and his words were a mess. He couldn't find them.

"Don't want *the*?"

"Don't want this all to fall apart before it even starts," he finally mumbled.

My breath hitched.

"Sorry, I'm a blunt person," Flynn said.

I nodded, even though he couldn't see me.

He kept going.

"Sorry, for taking this so qui—"

I laughed into the line. "Stop saying sorry."

"Sor—" je paused, letting out a small laugh. "I mean, whoops!"

"I'll see you tonight," I said softly, and he remained quiet for a couple seconds.

"I better. You better come," he said, but it sounded like he was telling himself that more than me.

"I will," I told him, my cheeks turning red.

"You *are*," he said confidently, and without uttering a bye, he ended the call. I remember loving the way he wanted me to come that night so bad, but now, I hated it. I hated the way he said all of it and I hated the way I fell for it all in a second. Because I didn't bother to fight it, I went along with every word and every action. Because I had always dreamed of the idea of someone wanting me, and when it finally happened, there was no way in hell I was pushing it all away just because of some gut feeling.

But maybe that's why I should have pushed it all away. Because it *was* a gut feeling.

* * *

"You don't want to dress too fancy, because it's not like you're going to a restaurant, but not too casual, considering this is a date," Liz said, shuffling through my closet and dresser for some clothes.

"Can I go with the romper?" I asked Liz, pointing at the black one with the ruffles at the end of the sleeves. I hadn't ever worn it, I was saving it. And maybe this was a good time to finally wear it.

"It showcases your long legs." Liz peered down, winking as I rolled my eyes and grabbed the romper off its hanger. I threw it at her face.

"Actually, I will save all the compliments so you can hear 'em from Flynn." Liz's lips curled upwards into a smirk, before she pushed me into the bathroom and raided my drawers for a make-up pallet and my hairbrush.

* * *

I pulled into his driveway, praying to God I got his address wrong and could spend another 10 pointless minutes distracting myself from getting to his house. *Was my dress too fancy? Or not fancy enough? Did I even look okay in it?*

Oh fuck, fuck-fuck-fuck. I was overthinking this entire thing. I couldn't strategically think my way through this. Love isn't math or science. There's no formula to it. It just happens when it happens. It was like I was trying to strategically formulate how this date would need to go for me to fucking earn a second date, so we could, I don't know, date?

I stepped out of the car and before I had even walked half way up his driveway, his front door whipped open, his eyes glossing across my entire body. I froze for a couple seconds. I felt warm and hot all over; he didn't mutter anything; he just stared. And I found myself loving it. I liked how he didn't have to say anything. I liked the way he looked at me.

Or maybe I just liked it because no one ever had.

"Hey," I muttered breathlessly, my gaze jumping around because I couldn't keep them on his face without breaking into some type of laugh.

His lips curled into a smile before he stepped out of the door. He weaved his hands through mine, gently pulling me into the door.

Chapter Six

His hand felt big and warm when they took over mine.

"Your hands are so small, I feel like I could break them," he finally spoke, and I tried to release my grip as the heat increased everywhere. He wouldn't let me let go. I raised my eyebrow, trying to push away the wrenching feeling I felt pool into my stomach.

"I'm serious, they're like butterfly wings. One touch, and it feels like they would break." For a couple seconds, I didn't think he was even talking about our hands.

"Anyways," I coughed as a blush painted his cheeks, he glanced down to the carpeted floor. His grip tightened. I didn't want him to let go. It made me feel something that I hadn't felt before. I didn't know if I liked it or was confused by it, but it made me feel *something*, and something was all I really needed.

Since he stopped mid-way through whatever he was going to say, I spoke instead.

"So, what's for dinner?"

"Actually, I was going to take you somewhere," Flynn said, and the way he said it made a warm gooey feeling pool into my stomach, causing a smile to break out on my face.

"A restaurant?" I asked.

His eyes gleamed, but he never gave me a solid reply, only shaking his head.

"Come on," he said.

Don't tell me just to come, uh, please exists?

"Uh, you don't just say it like that."

Flynn froze.

"How would you want me to say it then?" He almost sounded annoyed. I couldn't tell.

I turned away.

"It's gonna be fun," he finally muttered.

I just nodded my head.

He grabbed my hand again, his fingers curling alongside mine. I looked down at our hands merged together.

"You're coming, Ria."

I swallowed. "I am," I said, not liking the way I was already giving in. But the other part of me wanted to. *Really* wanted to.

"That's my girl," he said, a sly grin spreading across his face.

He noticed my reaction.

"You *will* be my girl," he mumbled, averting his gaze from anywhere but my face.

I wanted to push against him. *Your girl?* We don't even know each other. But I felt like whatever I said to him would be pointless. So I went with it. I nodded my head too eagerly. I gripped his hand too tightly. I went into his car with a grin on my face. I let go of all my relationship insecurities and trust issues and let him take me where he wanted to go to. I let his hand touch my thigh in the car. I let his arm wrap around my seat, and I held his hand the entire drive.

I let him do it all because I didn't want to push him away. Because no one had ever wanted to take me on a date. No one was ever so persistent about me coming on one with them. No one ever *saw* me. They saw straight through me. So I went along with every little thing he did, even if I didn't necessarily *like* it; it didn't make me not *want* any of it.

We pulled into a neighborhood about five minutes later.

I turned to face him, raising my eyebrow.

"Wow, what a nice restaurant. Good choice, good choice," I joked.

He rolled his eyes and his arm went across my body, glossing around my romper before unbuckling my seat belt.

"It's a party," he said, stepping out of the car.

"No shit."

He laughed then, the strange way he always did, and I huffed.

"So, you told me to trust you, and you take me to a party at basically…" I flail my hands around. "A frat house?" I finish.

He snorted. "That's hardly a frat house. Just come on. Live a bit."

I didn't reply but ended up following him into the house anyways. Flynn knocked on the door, I could make out the music and people yelling and I stepped back down a step. A young boy opened the door, his hands wrapped around a beer bottle as he leaned against the doorframe.

"Who's this one?" he asked, his tongue lapping across his lips as he eyed me up and down. I turned to look away, my hands weaving with one another.

"My girlfriend, Ria," he mumbled, and my head snapped. I didn't know if he said it to get into the party or if he said it because he meant it. What the fuck? I pushed Flynn's side, causing him to jolt. *God. Kill me now.*

The boy looked at me, his lips lifting up into a smirk.

"She doesn't seem to agree."

I didn't want to argue or start a fight, so I just went with it and nodded my head.

"Just another one?" the boy said to Flynn. What the fuck?

Flynn didn't reply for a few seconds. I noticed his gaze lowering to our hands.

"No."

The boy sighed, his fingers rummaging through his pocket to lift up a lighter.

"Yea, go in," he mumbled, not paying much attention and pulling open the door wider. Flynn gripped my hand. He was always doing this, like I was going to run away from him or leave him without a word.

"I'm not going anywhere," I mumbled, my cheeks heating up as I realized what I was saying.

"I know," he said. *He didn't.*

Flynn brought me to a small group of people, each one of them looked utterly wasted, and I didn't like this because it wasn't my scene. It was his. Flynn let go of my hand, and I breathed out when a girl started to make her way towards me.

"Want some?" A girl waved a bottle of pills in my face, and I backed up just as some guy crashed into my back. It was so loud. Crammed.

Flynn laughed, but it sounded nervous. He gripped my hand again.

"It's O, Ria." Flynn's fingers snaked around the girl's bottle. Her face broke into the strangest grin, and she stepped back and fell into the sofa behind her.

"I've never gotten high before," I admitted.

"You don't have to try it."

I looked around at everyone.

"Are you gonna?" I asked quietly, pointing to the bottle as the music in the house got louder.

Flynn thought for a second.

"It feels nice. Makes you forget things. Releases pain."

I swallowed. "I mean, if you will. I don't want to miss out." I said, curling my lips into a smirk just as he yanked the top of the bottle off.

"I don't want you to get addicted, become some addict like all of them. That's not you," Flynn told me, and I shook my head. Loving this new-found confidence. Wanting to try it. I always just stayed in my hole.

"You don't know me," I muttered breathlessly. Talking to him always left me draining—left me out of breath.

"I want to. And I will. *I will.*"

"Okay," was all I muttered, my eyes never leaving the bottle in his hands. He sounded so confident with himself, but I wasn't paying attention to what he was saying anymore. I rolled three pills around the palm of my hand, before breathing in and swallowing all three in one go.

* * *

Chapter Seven

It felt like time had just stopped. Or slowed down. I couldn't tell. Everything felt incredible and amazing and completely strange at the same time, like a numbing sensation that took me over. I had no thoughts. My mind was just running around. But I wasn't thinking. I turned to look at Flynn, who was struggling to walk towards me, tripping on vodka bottles that were scattered across the floor. He had a gleam in his eyes and I found myself laughing. I wasn't in control of anything and I loved it. Maybe if I wasn't on O I wouldn't have let Flynn do the things he did that night.

Because, before I knew it, he suddenly stood right in front of me. *I swear he was just down the hall.* My breath hitched. And then his thumb slowly glazed across my cheek and he moved closer towards me, gently cupping the nape of my neck. And then he stopped. I didn't want him to. I wanted it. So, I leaned in, eyes fluttering shut and pressed my lips against his without any hesitation. Losing time and thought altogether. And soon, his fingers gripped the edge of my top, fingers gliding against the skin below my belly button, and my fingers threaded his hair. *What was happening?* And maybe I should have stopped it. Maybe I should have told him that I met him two days ago and that this was going all too quick, but I didn't. Instead, my arms looped around his neck, in an effort to pull him as close as I could and my entire body felt hot all over. I pulled it away, stepping back into the wall, just as his fingers looped with mine, pulling me off the wall and forcing me to crash flush against him. He glanced down at me, and I noticed the way red spread across his cheeks.

"I like you. I don't know you that well, but I like you," Flynn said breathlessly, and for a couple seconds, I simply looked at him. I swallowed before saying my next words.

"I like you too."

His face broke into a smile.

"Good."

I didn't pay attention to anything he said. I just wanted to kiss him again. So I snaked my arms around his neck and did it all over again. I was never one to do stuff like this, especially with people watching. I wasn't me. I wasn't feeling like myself. And that's what I kept telling my head—this wasn't me, this wasn't Ria. I was just in the head of someone else for a bit.

"You kiss like I'm never gonna see you again," I mumbled, stepping back.

"That's the best way."

I laughed. And then he was chuckling. And then we were both drowning in the sound. I fell to the ground, laying on the side of the floor just as he bent down, his arm going under my waist. And then I remember my eyes piercing shut. The last thing I remember was someone throwing a bottle of beer to the wall and the sound of rap music playing in my ears.

* * *

When I woke up, I was back in my bedroom and for a couple minutes, I couldn't recall anything from the night before. It was like a bliss of emptiness. I lifted myself up and saw a folded paper near my lamp and curiously spread my fingers across the edge of the paper. I already felt giddy when I saw the signed name on the front of the paper.

HENNNRIIIIIEEEEETTTTTTTAAAAAA,

I giggled. *What the fuck.* I could already feel my cheeks turning red and he wasn't even here. *Fuck again.*

I managed to sneak your address from your friend, Liz. She seemed quite eager to give it to me; didn't mind at all when she had never even met me. True friend right there. Dropped you off here; No one in your family was home, I don't think. You look cute when you're asleep. Just cute in general. Also, you snore really loud; couldn't concentrate on driving! Text me.

Flynn.

You look cute when you sleep. Just cute in general. Oh, fuck.

Cute wasn't even an insane adjective or even descriptive in any sense at all. It's just, no one's ever complimented me before. Or even tried to. It made me feel obligated to like him even more. I lifted up my phone, checking the time because I had work. It got me out of the house and that was the only reason I applied for it. I had to arrive there by 9:30 am and it's for two hours, for four weeks. I murmured goodbye to my mom, who ignored me, (as always) and stepped outside. The summer wind kissed my bare shoulder, the cool air surrounding me as I slipped on my flats that my mom placed outside. I walked towards my Lexus before grabbing my keys and pulling at the door. I started the car and drove out of my driveway.

As the radio played, I hummed and tapped against the steering wheel. I turned into the lot, the large building filling my sight. I sighed, grasping the handle of my purse and exiting my car. I could feel myself getting nervous. I wanted to do something right and hoped that I could prove it to myself. I wanted to prove it to my dad.

I shook my head and walked towards the door. I stepped in and was greeted by a few men who worked there. They smiled at me and explained how I would organize some files for my first day. I didn't talk much, simply nodded my head and added a smile or two in there. They pointed me toward a door that had file storage for the different cars and wanted me to put them in their correct folders, alphabetically.

I nodded. Smiled politely. Repeated. And then I walked towards the room that one of the dudes pointed at. But my head was all over the place, and I couldn't care less about filing stupid papers when I couldn't stop thinking about last night.

Who was I?

I kissed him. He kissed me back.

No, Ria, File. Focus. And file. But I couldn't. I couldn't stop grinning the entire time. And I'm sure the employees thought I was insane, because I was organizing a mass of files with the widest smile across my lips. A good hour passed and I got the majority of them done before one of the men showed me around the building, explaining to me which cars were where, and the range of prices. The only thing keeping me going was getting that dang paycheck at the end of the day.

And then my mom called me. At first, I just wanted to let it ring and ring and ring until it hit voicemail, but for some reason, I sucked in a harsh breath and picked it up. I didn't let her talk first. I was going to get my words out before hers just took over.

"I'm at work, and I really can—" I started, lowering my voice.

"Ria, I know, I know, I wouldn't call you if I didn't nee -"

She always fucking calls me when she needs something. Never just to ask how my day's been. Or how my first day of work's gone. Or just, *anything.* I used to plan our conversations in my head of ones I wish me and Mom used to have.

"You always need something."

She sighed.

"I'm you're daughter, not your maid," I told her.

She breathed out.

"Exactly. You're my daughter and you're supposed to be here when I need you—"I cut her off because I couldn't *hear a*nything else.

"What about when I need you? What about when Dad gets drunk and I'm home alone, like, when I cried and you weren't here. When are you ever here?" I muttered, feeling the corner of my eyes itch with tears.

"Ria—"

"Yea, you're sorry. I know. It goes in one ear and out the other." I turned to see one of the workers walking towards me.

"I need you to talk to Dad…" she started, and I got worried she was going to start sobbing on the line and then I wouldn't be able to handle it, and I would drop everything to run to the house and hug her, but I just didn't want to this time.

"Am I some owl? If you need to talk to him, you do it. I don't want to be dragged into you guys' problems."

"Henrietta, you're part of the fam—"

"Fuck this family." I pressed my lips into a thin line when I realized my hands were slowly curling into fists.

My mom gasped against the line, and for a bit, she didn't reply, but she never left the call. Maybe I was being mean. But I was sick of false truths and making up crap to cover all the lies. I wanted her to know how I was feeling, how we all felt, because I was sick of falling into this never-ending rabbit hole of problems, *all, the, damn, time.*

I was over it.

"Please," my mom breathed, "come home." And without another word, she ended the call. I clenched my fists and furiously shoved my phone into my back pocket. All I could see was red. Red everywhere, just burning me.

Come home?

HOME?

Someone tell me where that is.

Before I could stay mad for more than a hot second, I turned to face the entrance door to see Jon trudging towards me, and in seconds, that frown twisted into a small smile.

Chapter Eight

"Liz made me drive all the way to Chipotle just to get food for your dumb ass," Jon rolled his eyes passing me the bag, and I grinned.

"Send Liz my love," I teased as I opened the bag.

"And, *me*? The one who drove?"

"Oh yea, forgot about you," I said with a glint in my eyes, tearing apart the lid.

"Long love my friends," Jon muttered and I threw the bag at his face.

"Where's Liz?" I asked him, giving him a fork so he could share the bowl with me.

"At the library, finishing up Vassar College apps and obviously having a panic attack," Jon said.

I sighed.

"Why won't she get she's gonna do fine? 3.9's gonna get her into lots of places," I muttered, stuffing food into my mouth.

"Also, she wanted me to ask for you. How did your little night out go?" Jon's lips curled upwards into a smirk and I turned away, rolling my eyes. There was no way in hell I could tell him what happened. *Oh yea, so I got high for the first time in my life, got drunk, and made out with a guy I literally met two days ago!*

"It was alright," I said, almost laughing at how bad the lie was. *Alright*. I couldn't find a word to describe what the fuck happened last night, because even I didn't understand what had happened. I still don't.

"You lost it, didn't you?"

"Oh my God, Jon, I am not having this fucking conversation with you," I said as I turned away, not meeting his gaze because of my face.

"*Fucking* conversation, huh?" Jon winked, and my cheeks started to burn. Damn it.

"Screw you," I mumbled under my breath.

"But, that's what Flynn did to you!" Jon's grin was growing wider and wider with each second, so I just ended up throwing the bag of Chipotle at his face, before flipping him off and leaving the building with a laugh.

I hadn't called Flynn back. I kept checking my phone to see if he called or texted, and he did. I didn't want to open it yet, which I don't get, because I'm the one who wants the call? I just felt so confused.

I remember, three days later, I never called him back. Mom took away my phone because she caught me yelling at Elaine; it wasn't, like, my choice. I wanted to call him, but he took it the wrong way and that was the first sign. But I was just blind by want.

"You never answered my calls." He came running up the driveway. I started to laugh.

I gently pushed his shoulder.

"Silly, it's been three days."

I glanced back at my door. He was about to open his mouth, but my words flew out before his.

"My mom took my phone, I'm sorry." Why the hell was I apologizing? I didn't do anything wrong. It's not like we're dating. He's just a dude I kissed. Yea, *dude*. I like that word.

He shook his head, gently pushing his finger under my chin and lifting my head up.

"You got me worried," he muttered breathlessly.

I smiled at him, pressing my lips to the side of his cheek and stepping back with a triumphant look on my face.

"Hey, you can't just the kiss the cheek to act like —"

I shook my head, smirking lightly.

"Sorry, you can get your *presents* later." A flash of something went across his eyes, but it was gone so fast I couldn't even tell if it happened. I would have asked him. But fights and arguments scared me. But what I didn't realize was, that was the way of a relationship. The ones that make it work go through everything, and they get through it. That's the beauty of it.

I wanted him to stay and I knew he did too, but I wasn't ready for him to see what it was like in my house. Little did I know that he knew better than anyone else.

"Can I come in?" he asked me, eying the house. I turned back.

"Uhm, it's not mine," I muttered, trying not to look at him.

"What do you mean?" He tried to glance down the door. I gripped his arm. I knew I could distract him.

"It's my friends, Liz. SAT prep." *God, that stupid test made its way to every fucking conversation.*

"You don't sound so sure," he muttered, and I mentally punched myself because I had no idea how he could even tell. I think that's what drew me towards him in the first place. He could always just *tell*. I didn't have to say anything or do anything. He knew.

I laughed, but I feared it came off shaky.

"Don't worry, it's just Liz."

Flynn looked at me for a bit and I knew my cheeks were red, so I looked away, bringing my hand to the back of my neck.

"Call me. Text me. Just…" Flynn paused, eyes on anything but my face. "Just talk to me." His voice was turning quiet, like he was scared. I just didn't get how scared he was the entire time.

I merely nodded my head, but before I could even conjure up some reply, he took his bike and was off.

* * *

"The fucking rain knocked the power out," Jon muttered, aimlessly walking into my house with his friend Charleston. Charleston was this guy Liz had a crush on all of middle school. She conjured up the courage to ask him to the 8th grade dance, where she lost her first kiss, and then he just never spoke to her again.

"Who said he was invited?" Liz glared at Jon, who eyed Charleston with the harshest glare and I just laughed. Like, that was way back, she should be over it now.

"Invited to what? This ain't some party. It's a house with no lights on."

"No lights equals party." Charleston's lips grew into a smirk and I shoved him towards the door.

"The door is that way," I pointed, realizing it was completely dark and *I* didn't even know where the door was.

"You're stupid," he mumbled.

Just as I was about to point towards the left side, the door flew open and in walked Elaine and Brian. She was smiling, her hands molded with his and I couldn't stop the grin from flying to my face. Seeing people I love happy, makes me 10 times happier even if I am drowning in sobs.

"The power's out," Charleston told her.

I rolled my eyes.

"And you calling *m*e stupid? No shit."

"Where's Dad?" Elaine asked me, walking down the hallway but tripping every two seconds. She always asked me that. Sometimes, even if she did know where he was. Even if he was in the kitchen, she would still ask me where he was. It took me so long to comprehend what she was asking. Where is Dad, really. I think we lost him a long time ago. We lost him when he lost Mom.

I shrugged my shoulders. Sometimes, I tell myself if I just stop caring, then maybe, I just eventually won't. I don't want to care. I don't want to worry about him. I'm his daughter. I'm not his mom. But then I'm *always* worried about them.

"Like I would know. It's not like he calls. Or texts. Or even talks." The house grew silent, and I realized I might crack with everyone just watching me. I rolled my eyes, forcing the corner of my lips to curl into a small smile. Elaine didn't reply. She just kept walking until she crashed into the couch, yanking Brian down with her with a giggle.

Ah, young love. Too cute.

I was just so obsessed with the idea of it all—falling in love—that when it did happen, I couldn't even tell. I envied how happy Elaine was sometimes, and I hated that. It's why I wanted *a* Flynn so bad. It's why, when he came, I didn't push it away. It's why even if my feelings weren't true, I kept him and destroyed him at the same time.

"She wouldn't stop talking about the dance," Charleston said.

I turned to look at him.

"Some people like dances, it lets them fit in,*" I was talking about myself.* I couldn't see his face in the dark, I was glad. I didn't want to see his reaction.

"Oh, really?"

I shrugged. Even though he couldn't see me.

He came closer. I could feel his breath fanning my face and I stepped back.

"Let her live. She's 16," I said.

"Seems to me you really like dances too."

I shook my head.

"Never been to one so I don't care." I muttered.

"Never been to one, or never asked?"

Liz came up to him, grabbing his shoulders.

"God, you're such an ass."

Charleston's face fell.

"You used to like this ass."

Liz snorted.

"In the, um, 8th grade? And yea, I know. Biggest regret of my life."

"You still did," he said.

Liz rolled her eyes. That, I could see.

"Yea, well you weren't a total dick then. Some people grow up. And some people just change for the worse."

* * *

Chapter Nine

"*You're* picking him up?" Liz asked me disapprovingly.

I shrugged.

"He doesn't have his license," I muttered, realizing how stupid I sounded. I'm 17, driving my 18-year-old *boyfriend, dude, thing*, to our date. Don't guys normally plan these types of things?

"He's 18?"

Okay, maybe it was a bit weird.

"Okay, I don't really mind driving him."

"It's just sketchy," Liz mumbled, turning away.

"You don't even know him, and weren't you the one that encouraged me to go for him in the first place?"

Liz shrugged, not meeting my eyes.

"Well, I personally don't think it's that big of a deal for me to drive him places," I told her, staring to get annoyed. She was almost being judgmental. She was the one who had him drive us home when we knew him for less than 3 seconds. Oh my God, we let him drive us and he didn't have his license.

"Okay then, as long as you don't mind it, but just... I don't know. Maybe you were right. We don't really know him," Liz said.

"Exactly. We don't. What do you think I'm trying to do?"

* * *

I pulled into his driveway. He was waiting for me on his porch. He opened the door, slid in his seat and in seconds, had his lips on mine and hands in my hair.

"Thanks for picking me up," Flynn murmured, pulling away. I smiled, looking at my blind spot.

"It's just I can't get a bus ti—"

I cut him off. I wanted to know more about him. "Why?"

He didn't reply to me. He kept going. "*Ticket.* So it was nice *you* could."

"You could always take the bus," I urged him on.

"Fee is expensive."

I laughed at that. I shouldn't have.

"It's only a dollar 50! I can give you 10 bucks because it sucks walking everywhere," I told him.

He turned his head, his face small and red. "I could never take your money."

I cracked a smile. "It's just 10 bucks. Don't be afraid to ask."

"I don't want you to be my bank," Flynn murmured softly.

I scoffed. "Flynn, it's 10 bucks. Really, it's nothing. Honestly, I feel worse not giving you more."

"10 bucks would be so much for me," he said quietly, turning away from me and facing the window. I wanted to ask him what he meant. But part of me already knew. I just wanted to know the story. I realized Flynn never mentioned his family ever. And then I remembered they had no cars. My face softened.

"I haven't even said anything and you're already giving me the 'I feel bad' face," Flynn said, shaking his head.

"I can't help myself. I just feel like it's gonna be bad," I said, my fingers tightening on the wheel.

"Yea, well, nobody's lives are perfect. There's just too many holes that can't be filled," he muttered. Noticing the way my face changed, his fingers snaked around mine in seconds. I wanted to pull away. Because that's what it felt like he was doing. But I stood still, letting him pull us closer.

"I get you on that," I replied a few seconds later.

I was worried his jaw would clench or he would get mad, revolt, and be all 'how would you know' and shit, but he didn't. And I loved that. He just, understood.

"I know you do."

"Want some froyo?" I asked him, trying to change the mood and force my face to turn into a smile, because I hated the feeling that we were having in the car.

"I don't have money."

I never took that the three different ways it could be taken. I just laughed and gripped his shoulders causing him to shake lightly.

"I can pay, silly."

It looked like he wanted to say something else, but he just stepped forward, gripped my chin and molded our lips together with a smile.

Chapter Ten

As we walked in, he started asking questions. I glanced at the different flavors.

He asked: Have you had a boyfriend?

To which I replied: No, I haven't.

He raised a brow.

He said: Huh.

I said: Yep. Why?

He said: I'm shocked. I get you before anyone else.

I gripped his side, for some reason, my fingers were trembling. I just felt so overwhelmed. But I couldn't let him see me cry, so I just asked him questions.

"What about you?"

"Have I ever had a boyfriend?" he teased me, and I almost froze until he started laughing.

"I've had two girlfriends, but here, nothing to you."

I could only scoff. "You've known me for less than two weeks," I said, grabbing a plastic cup for the yogurt and handing it to him. He merely shrugged.

"Sometimes that's all you need." Flynn grinned, telling the guy at the counter which toppings he wanted. *Sometimes.*

"Yes, the cherry," he said as I pointed to the animal crackers.

"God, I used to have those crackers so much when I was younger. Mom never gets them anymore," I said, my heart clenching at the mere mentioning of her. I hated it. Why couldn't I let a day pass without me acting five with that name?

"You talk about your mom so strangely, like she isn't here anymore," Flynn said, staring ahead.

I almost choked.

"She's been gone for so long," I said in a quiet voice.

"She's still here, she's just been missing for a bit." I didn't want to talk about my mom, so I forced a smile on my lips as I practically sipped on the yogurt.

"Coming from a true writer," I said with a smile, making a grin spread across his lips.

"It's honestly the only thing I'm half decent at," he mumbled.

I put my hand on his shoulder.

"Writing is good. I think the way writers think is so complex. They just see the world in so many ways."

Flynn smiled again.

"Tell my dad that." This was the first time he had mentioned his dad, but I didn't want to push him about anything so I just wrapped my hands around his waist and tugged him closer. He didn't budge. I lifted my head off his chest. I was always so scared to say certain things around him; like I controlled myself from saying how I actually felt or what I actually believed.

"This is the part where you, you know, return the damn hug," I muttered into his shirt, taking in his cologne. God damn. His chest vibrated with that laugh and I wanted to hear that sound on repeat all the time.

We sat down at one of the tables and ended up just sharing one bowl of the yogurt, mixing our flavors because we both liked what the other picked out. He took the spoon out of my mouth, licking the leftover yogurt off it with a sly grin.

"That's rude," I stuck my tongue out at him, trying to grab the spoon from his grasp, but he was too quick. In the end, I took the bowl at his face and stood up, preparing to exit and preparing for him to follow me out.

I finally had someone who would do that. I would leave. And he wouldn't let me go alone. I turned back to see and he was running after me, wrapping his arms around my waist and lowering his lips towards the shell of my ear. I shivered. But not because I was cold. I was so nervous when he was that close.

"Does it scare you?" he blurted. *You this close? Yes.*

"What does?"

"That I lik—" he paused, like he was thinking through what he was about to say. Instead of saying anything, he put his head on top of mine.

"When you lose so many people, you just think they're all gonna leave," he started and I swallowed. I never knew what to say to anything he ever said.

"I'm taking gibberish, ignore me."

I shook my head.

"You never talk gibberish. Stop making it seem like what you say doesn't matter."

"Yea b—"

I pressed my lips into a small line.

"You have a mouth. Use it."

"Guess I will," he murmured, pecking my lips in a swift motion.

My phone rang and I didn't want to answer it. I hugged myself before yanking the device out of my pocket to see Elaine calling me, and I pressed the answer button within a second. If it was anyone else, I wouldn't have even bothered picking it up.

I couldn't even manage to get a word out before Brian started on the line, his voice laced with confusion and pure panic.

"Ria?" he kept repeating my name, quicker each time.

"Yea?" I pushed my phone into my ear, trying to hear what was in the background. I could already feel my fingers beginning to shake. I could already tell something was wrong and Brian had only said my name.

"It's Elaine, I don't know what the fuck is happening. She's having some sort of panic attack and breathing fast and cryi—"

"Where are you two?" I breathed out, rummaging through my bag for my keys.

"Your house. Your dad's here too," Brian muttered, his voice growing quieter.

I closed my eyes.

"Fuck," I muttered. I didn't say bye. I ended the call and started to leave the store. I didn't even realize I was in my car without saying bye to Flynn or even bothering to give him a ride. It was like my entire mind just turned off. I was only focused on Elaine.

* * *

Chapter Eleven

I didn't realize how far I was from home until I got there. I saw Brian's car. And Dad's. But not Mom's. I unlocked my front door, ignoring the constant ringing from my phone, and stepped inside. So carefully and so slowly, as if the house was about to burn down.

And then Elaine came running down the stairs and, in seconds, had her arms wrapped around me and her head stuffed in my neck. I stepped back.

"Elaine, what the hell happened?" I asked quietly.

She remained still.

"Dad, he said he wants to leave, and I guess I just exploded."

I breathed out.

He can't leave. Not after everything. He promised. He promised he would stay. Guess a promise is just the same as anything else he says. The words just lost its meaning.

"What did you do?"

She gripped my hand, letting go of my waist. Brian walked into the hallway with a sad smile on his lips, his hands sifting through his locks.

"She didn't just explode. She went bat-shit crazy." I raised my brow, glancing down at Elaine who released a long sigh.

"What the fuck did she do?"

Elaine glanced up.

"Look, I just cracked, okay? I had so much to say to him after he said he wants to leave. He told me he's been planning it for months. He told me he had been planning to leave for months. He had it all worked out. The date. How he was gonna do it. He was gonna go without saying a fucking BYE, Ria." Elaine spluttered out.

My body was frigid.

The only thing running in my head was that I had just spoken to Dad a couple days ago, he told me he was going to work it out with Mom. What the fuck.

I placed my hand on my forehead.

"He's such a liar. He knew all this time. All that BS on marriage, and fights, and love was complete bullshit, because it doesn't fucking exist." I started up the stairs, my body moving before my head. Elaine tried to grab my hand, attempting to pull me down the stairs, but I wanted—no, *needed*—to go up and hear what he had to say.

I just want this all to end. I just want to know everything. I needed to understand.

"He won't tell me why. You won't get it out of him," Elaine told me, but everything I could see was red.

"I need to try. If I don't, I won't ever forgive myself."

Brian glanced out the front door window, and I caught the confusion slide across his frame.

I ran up. Dad's car was gone.

"How did he E—"

Elaine pointed at the back door.

"He's such a fucking child! Is he 7 or 43? This isn't the third grade," I muttered. *He can't even face us.* I just don't get what happened to him. He used to be the way a *dad* was. He would show up to my soccer games. He would always be the one cheering the loudest. I could make out his voice from the field. He would be the one I would go to whenever I needed help with, just, *anything.*

It feels like the polar opposite now.

"Is he running away...?" Elaine swallowed and I shook my head. I pointed to the desk with his phone and wallet; he can't go without packing a bag.

I laughed, despite the whole situation. "He can't leave without those."

My phone was ringing and I yanked it out to see my 7th missed call from Flynn, and I didn't want to answer it so I just turned my phone off instead.

"You know what? We're going swimming," I started, attempting to force a smile on my lips. Maybe if I just kept smiling, eventually one would appear without me forcing it. I wanted a distraction, a way to forget the shit that just happened. I didn't even care if I would have to deal with this an hour later. I wanted to put all this *on hold.*

"We're on pause for the rest of the night," I blurted.

Brian turned around, his brows raising in turmoil.

"Like, I want us to not worry about what just happened. I want to pretend we're on a pause. I don't want anyone crying or frowning. I don't want anyone thinking about what just happened. I want us to talk about other things for the rest of the night, and we can un-pause in a few hours," I said. I used to do this when me and Liz got into fights. We would just pretend nothing happened and worry about it when we were *ready* to worry about it.

I thought Elaine would look at me like I was crazy, but she nodded her head and went off to find swimwear. Sometimes, putting things on hold makes it seem like they don't exist. It makes everything feel simpler. I grabbed my cell and called Liz.

"Hey, hey, we're going night swim—"

"Hell yes," Liz laughed.

I smiled into the line.

"Invite *him!*" Liz said, and I shook my head.

"Fuck, I never gave him a ride. I have to call him, I'm so stupid, Liz. He can't drive and I left him somewhere, alone. I gotta go, see yoooouuuuu." I ended the call just as my fingers glossed across his contact name on my phone. I didn't even realize it, I mean, I may have, but it was like my mind just turned off and I simply didn't care.

So, I called him before I would think myself out of it and he picked up on the first ring. Fuck, I muttered quietly.

"Hey," he whispered, his voice barely audible.

"I'm so so sorry for leaving you alone at that place. My sister called and I—" I started, just as he cut me off.

"Look," I could make out someone else in the background, their voice only raising in both sound and tone.

"Hey, is everything alrigh—"

"I gotta go. I'll call you tomorrow," Flynn mumbled, before ending the call so abruptly. I felt my chest tighten. The way he was talking, he wasn't himself and I could tell, even though I've known for him such a little amount of time. I released a breath I never realized I was holding, just as Elaine appeared by the stairs and I turned around, forcing a smile on my face.

On pause.

"Finally get a point to try this baby on," Elaine said, her fingers curling around the straps of the bathing suit and me and Brian rolled our eyes.

"I'm just not even bringing a bathing sui—" I started with a grin, and then Liz stepped inside with gleaming eyes.

"If you're stripping, call your boyfriend."

I rolled my eyes, feeling my cheeks turn hot and warm.

"He's *no*t my boyfriend," I muttered.

Liz looked at me as a smirk pulled at the corner of her lips.

"Alright, call your dude that you kissed."

"He's *not my dude*," I mumbled under my breath.

"He will be sooooooon." Liz winked at me, just as Brian and Elaine laughed, and I sat there, pondering over the whole conversation. He was my first kiss. I think that makes him more than just a dude. But I was sick of even thinking about it, so I pushed it away, pretending I had no problems in relation to anything and nothing mattered.

"Does it take you five months to put on your shoes?" Liz said as her head peeked through the hole in the door. I let out a laugh while shaking my head, and then ran out to the car, forgetting about my shoes altogether.

* * *

Chapter Twelve

"You know if the police come..." Jon started as I grabbed the keys from my back pocket. I shook my head with a laugh. At this point, I don't think I really care.

"Nah, I got a key. I'll just say I work here," I said.

"Good plan," Liz teased as I pushed the key into the hole, starting to turn it.

Before the door was fully opened, Elaine and Brian managed to slip inside and had already placed their bags on seats. I watched her face break into grins that covered her whole face, and she eagerly jumped into the pool as my eyes wandered around to see if anyone else was here. I wanted more of these moments. Where it felt like time had frozen and nothing mattered, because I just didn't care. And maybe I should, but I didn't want to.

"Well, thanks for inviting me." I turned around to see Charleston and I rolled my eyes.

"This wasn't something we really planned," I mumbled.

Charleston yanked his shirt off, staring out at the pool.

"You know, if the police come, this is all y—""

I huffed. "You know, I'm not the only damn person in this room. You all are."

Charleston cracked a grin.

"I'm teasing, breathe, breathe."

"Don't *Breathe* me." I rolled my eyes, suddenly self-conscious that he was right beside me as I was taking off my clothes. Maybe I should just swim in these, I thought, glancing down at my penguin pajama pants and Dad's white shirt I stole from him a few weeks ago.

It was the one with the stain from the... no, no, *pause.*

Charleston jumped into the pool and I decided to just stick with my clothes.

"Where's your boyfriend?" he asked, pulling his head out of the water.

I stuck my tongue out at him.

"Why does everyone keep asking that?"

Charleston shrugged in the water.

"It's funny to see you turn red."

I flipped him off as my fingers snaked around the elastic of my shorts and I yanked them down, thanking God I was wearing my dad's shirt that was three times larger than me.

"Okay, maybe when someone actually likes you, you might get embarrassed sometimes too," I mumbled as I jumped into the pool, holding my nose.

"Bitch," Charleston muttered, and I laughed, jumping around the water and attempting to swim towards Liz.

We were barely in the pool for 10 minutes before I heard a police siren in the distance. We dipped out of the recreation center but the policeman already saw us, shook his head, and put us in his car. He gave us a long lesson on breaking in, and we all just sat in silence nodding our heads, because no one wanted to say anything. We got to the police department and he led us into the waiting room.

"I better not catch you kids doing something like that again. Just wait here." We all nodded our heads and sat in the room, waiting for my parents who weren't even answering their phones. And then I saw Flynn at the entrance desk, talking to a lady. His voice was quiet but strained, like he was trying hard not to yell.

I stood up and started walking towards him. He didn't notice.

"I need to talk to someone," he said.

The lady didn't even glance up from her computer.

"What's the emergency?" Flynn didn't respond. Instead, he stepped back and shook his head.

"It's nothing important," he whispered, his eyes on the ground. And the lady nodded her head before helping the person behind Flynn.

"Hey you," I said when he finally turned around, his eyes widened.

"What are you doing here?" I asked him, watching the way he wouldn't meet my eyes.

"Someone broke into the house. But it's fine, they took things that didn't even matter," he said.

Ignoring anything else, he shook his head.

"Now let's get you and your friends out of here for whatever you did." The corner of his lips lifted upwards into a smile and I grinned.

Chapter Thirteen

"Fuck, thank you," I mumbled into his shirt as his chest vibrated with laughter.

"I think four thank yous is good."

I pulled back a bit, glancing up with a sad smile growing on my face. I pulled him towards me into another hug, where I simply lingered for far more then I needed to. But I loved the feeling of being wrapped around his arms, and I didn't want it to leave.

"Come on, let's get you home," he mumbled into my hair.

I pulled back.

"I owe you, let me drive you." Flynn immediately froze and gripped my hand so tightly, I thought it would just break with his tight grip.

"You drove me before." His teeth were clenched. I ate the lump in my throat.

"It's okay, Flynn, it's late, really—" I started, not realizing the way my voice was going quieter with each word.

Flynn curled his hands into fists.

"I insist," he started with a strained voice. "Let me drive you home."

"Are you alright?" I stopped my sentence midway.

I didn't want to say anything. I didn't want to fight back. I hated arguments. I was always that person who would say sorry to someone, where it wasn't even my fault, because I wanted to end them.

So, I simply nodded my head and walked out of the station with him, without another word back.

I couldn't tell what he was thinking. Most of the time, it's easy for me to tell exactly what people are thinking because they show it. But Flynn doesn't, really.

"What happened earlier?" I asked softly as he reached over and buckled my seatbelt, his arm briefly grazing across my waist, lingering there for longer than needed.

He didn't say anything. Silence was louder than most words, especially in his case. When it was quiet, it answered everything, and the silence was all I needed to figure Flynn out.

"You're not much of a talker are you," I said, facing the window.

He turned towards me, his eyes, face, cheeks, glowing.

"Nah, I use my lips for limited purposes," Flynn said, winking at me. But I didn't crack a smile. Maybe I should have asked him there what happened. Maybe I should have showed him I cared. He wanted me to, he just didn't know how to say it.

"My dad left," I mumbled, pressing my face into my hands.

I watched his fingers tighten around the wheel, redness crawling up towards his fingertips.

"I wish mine would," Flynn uttered as he adjusted his shirt.

"When they actually do, you won't want that," I said. I've told my dad to leave so many times, and now that he's left—even temporarily—I hate it. I want him back. Even if he never was really here, I want him in the house, just to know he's there. He was still my dad, and no matter how much I dislike him, he's family, and that won't ever change.

You can't undo family.

Flynn pulled off the road as his face rapidly turned to look at me and his eyes bored with mine.

"You want to take E?" He asked me, his eyes quickly searching my face.

I practically choked,

"What the hell?"

He started rummaging through his bag and I watched the way his trembling fingers snaked around a small bag filled with white pills.

"You're mad about your dad. Have some."

I shook my head. I turned to look out the window. The sky was a black sheet.

"I'm not just going to take drugs, not right now," I muttered, turning to face him.

"Flynn, let me drive you home," I continued. My voice growing quieter with every passing second.

"You took them fine a week ago."

My chest burned.

"Well, I don't want to now," I said quietly.

Flynn put his head on the wheel and I noticed his chest was rapidly rising up and down. I stood still, my fingers itching to wrap my arms around him. Instead, I held his hand.

"Come on, lemme take you home," I said, and he kept shaking his head.

"I can't go home. I can't go home," Flynn kept repeating, his voice low and barely audible.

I sighed.

"Come on, please. You can go home and sleep," I told him.

"*Home,*" He mumbled.

I should have realized right there that something was up, but I didn't. I was too scared to push him. I just wanted to get along with him.

"What about your mom? I can take you to her," I said.

His face flew up.

"No, no," he breathed out. I curled my fingers around his. I just didn't know what else to do. I was always scared to say anything; scared I would say the wrong thing.

"You can stay with me until you're ready to go home," I murmured softly, and he looked at me with a sad smile before mumbling...

"I don't think I ever will be."

* * *

"It's this one," I said quietly, pointing towards my house as we pulled into the driveway. Flynn got out of the car without a word. He started walking up the driveway, his steps slow, as if they were planned.

"Is anyone home?" Flynn asked me.

I shrugged my shoulders.

"Guess we'll find out."

Flynn said nothing, he just looked at me. I pulled the door open, taking in a deep breath and flipping the light switch on. Before I could even glance around the halls to see if anyone was home, Flynn's arms were quick to wrap themselves around my waist, tugging me towards him until we were chest to chest. My breaths came out slow with my heart shaking in my chest.

He kissed me then, slow and sweet. His fingers crept upwards, lingering on my waist and my stomach. His finger curled around the hem of my tee shirt, but I didn't stop him, I smiled into his lips before pulling away with a small smirk.

"Let's watch some movies," I said, going into the living room.

"You can't just leave me like that," Flynn mumbled with red cheeks.

I turned around with a wink. "Movies," I said.

"Where are your' parents?" He asked me, but I just… cracked.

"Where are yours?" I fought back. Watching his face fall, I sighed and walked towards him.

"I'm sorry," I breathed. "It's just, you ask so many questions about my family and don't let me ask about yours."

He laughed then.

"You can always ask," Flynn started, a small glint playing in his eyes. "Doesn't mean I have an answer."

I shook my head.

"Why do you want to know?" he asked.

I averted my eyes from his face.

"I just…" I began. "Never mind."

"The hard part is, sometimes I don't even have an answer, because *I* don't know. I don't get my family. I don't know them."

I walked to the shelf with some films.

"It's okay, you don't need to tell," I said in a hushed tone. He grew closer, and suddenly, I was reminded of the E he asked me to take in the car. I shook my head. *That wasn't him.* It was just an excuse in my head. I wanted to make him feel perfect. In my head, he was. But that was because I created someone completely different there. I was too scared of the truth. Too scared to admit it to myself.

I rummaged through the piles of DVD's, before grabbing 4 and throwing them to Flynn on the couch, who patted the space beside him.

Chapter Fourteen

I walked towards him without a word, grabbing the blanket and throwing it over myself. I wasn't sure how close I should get to him, and I'm sure he realized the way my breaths turned heavy and I turned quiet. I was barely meeting his gaze. I just stared at the TV screen, even though there was no movie playing.

I noticed he moved a bit in an attempt to get closer. *Why was I so afraid? I already got the kiss out of the way.*

"You're nervous," Flynn stated, releasing a sigh.

I said nothing, pretending I wasn't paying attention because I was distracted by the movie.

His knees briefly touched mine. When I sucked in a breath, he scooted away, but his touch continued to linger seconds after. I didn't know why I was practically shaking, not at the time at least. I turned to face him, to see his eyes were closed and he had sunk into the back of the couch. Without really thinking, my eyelashes fluttered shut and I moved backwards. My hair sprawled across his chest. I didn't stop it. I turned to face the couch and fell asleep to the sound of his short breaths and hammering chest.

* * *

My phone read 1:33 a.m., and as I lifted myself up, I realized I was laying on the couch instead of Flynn. I flipped the lights on and when I looked through the window, I saw my dad's car. And for a couple seconds, my lips grew into a smile. It didn't stay like that for long. I ran around the house and searched all the rooms for my dad, but I couldn't find him. Or Flynn. Why the hell was I always looking for my dad?

In parts of my head, I figured Flynn might leave. I wish my dad stayed. But he was as gone as Flynn was.

My head was spinning. I texted Flynn. I called him. I left countless voicemails. No response. I texted my dad. I called him. I left even more voicemails then I did for Flynn. No reply.

Grabbing my keys, I walked towards the door. I didn't know what I was even doing. All I knew was I was sleeping beside Flynn, and I wake up, and he's not there. I didn't know where to go. I think I was just hoping I would drive around and eventually see him, just walking down a block or some weird shit.

I drove out of the driveway with my fingers trembling as they gripped the wheel. I turned the radio on. I didn't want to hear my head.

I tapped at the wheel as I anxiously raked the sidewalks in my neighborhood. I didn't think he would just leave my house to stroll around my neighborhood. He must be going somewhere. And then I see Elaine at the corner of a streetlight, sitting on the edge of a curb, with her hands curling through her hair.

I almost didn't stop the car. I thought maybe she wanted space. Maybe she didn't want to talk. But before my mind could transition into other thoughts, I turned the car towards her. She didn't move at all. She didn't bring her head up. It was like she expected me to be here.

"Elaine?"

She didn't answer.

Instead of saying anything else, I sat beside her, snaked my arms around her waist, and put my head on her shoulder.

"Go find Dad," Elaine finally muttered, standing up so casually.

I stood up too.

"Go home," I said.

"I can't. Not until you... we find him."

"Okay."

Elaine walked towards the door and pulled open the passenger door. I watched her as she glanced behind her, her fingers wiping at her eyes.

"Flynn's gone too," I said.

"Who the fuck cares about him right now? Your *dad* is missing."

"So is my boyfriend?"

Elaine scoffed, "*Boyfriend*?"

I turned the car on.

"Just find Dad first. You can look for Flynn on your own time," Elaine muttered, facing the window.

"Jesus, okay," I mumbled.

"Don't *Jesus* me. Dad's gone. Missing. Not home. Gone."

I sighed. "Yea, I fucking know that."

"Then why don't you act like it matters? You're making it seem like him just missing isn't affecting you."

I shook my head.

"He's *my dad*. It affects me whether I want it to or not. He's done this type of thing before, you know," I said.

I turned out of the neighborhood.

"Where are you going?" Elaine asked.

I shrugged my shoulders.

"The night club, the one down the block. He goes there a lot. What's to say he won't be there again?"

* * *

I parked down the block, yanking the car door open just as Elaine stepped out.

"Elaine, stay in the car."

She shook her head.

"I'm coming in. I want to see his face when I walk in," she said firmly.

"Elaine..."

She looked at me for a bit, and swallowed a lump in her throat before going back in the car. I couldn't help my chest rising up and down so quickly. My breaths were turning heavy and long. I lifted out my ID and walked inside.

I didn't pay attention to anyone else. I was more focused on Flynn than my dad. My dad was an adult. He could take care of himself. I was his child, I shouldn't be spending so much time taking care of him, acting like the parent. I handed the bartender my ID. He glanced up and down, and I'm sure he knew I was underage, but he let me in either way.

I watched him continue to stare at me as I walked off, and I suddenly got self-conscious. I yanked my cardigan down and over my butt. My eyes quickly scanned the bar stools and then, I suddenly saw Dad—sitting on one of the stools, a glass in his hand. His fingers were tightly snaked around it, and even from a distance, I could see the redness climb up his fingers. I stood frozen. My head was running with a million thoughts and I wanted to say a million different things, but my mouth stayed shut and I stayed still. I watched him for a bit.

He had no idea I was there. The bar was completely crowded and it was so loud, but for some reason, it didn't feel like that. It felt silent. It felt like there were only three people in the room and not 90.

I stopped paying attention to Dad for a couple minutes and eyed the people I was surrounded with. I lost my thoughts when my favorite song played.

When I turned back to Dad, I saw Flynn and my jaw dropped, and my body started moving through the crowd in an instant.

Chapter Fifteen

He had passed out.

I don't remember this night as vividly as I want to, nothing from it really made any sense. Why Flynn was there in the first place. He could have chosen to go anywhere, but he chose the bar and so did my dad. I didn't understand why Dad didn't just fight his problems and not try to just forget them. Maybe that's where I get it from.

It seemed I just didn't understand anything.

I shoved people aside and I guess my dad could tell it was me, because he turned around with wide eyes, his hands trembling around Flynn's hands.

"Call fucking 911!" I was yelling at the bartender. My dad stood still.

"Why aren't you doing anything? What the hell happened to him?"

My dad's eyes shut.

He was about to lie, I knew it.

"He just passed out."

"No one just fucking passes out," I said with my teeth clenched. I could hear the ambulance in the distance, and my heartbeat escalated.

My dad stood up, his legs falling apart under him. I wanted to laugh. I wanted to scream at him until my voice was ripped out of my lungs. But I just stared down at him.

"I'm sorry," my dad whispered, his voice cracking.

"Don't you cry," I said, my eyes averted from his face but facing the window. The ambulance pulled up, I rushed towards them, pointing them towards Flynn. After that, everything became a mess and a blur.

Flynn was sent to the hospital that night. I didn't know why until two weeks later. Dad never let me visit him. He wouldn't tell me why. A week went by without me seeing him. A whole two weeks. I didn't realize how heavy I felt. How lonely. It didn't matter that I had Liz. *I wanted him.* He made me feel so many things, so many emotions I wanted to feel all the time. Even if I acted like I was scared of them. I loved it.

"Stop moping around. It's not like he went off to college and is visiting after a year, it's been like two weeks," Liz said, wandering around my kitchen.

"Two weeks too long."

Liz rolled her eyes.

"He's in the frickin' hospital! He could have died."

"He was released the following day, Liz. I'm worried sick. I don't know what the hell happened to him. He left my house, went to a bar, passed out, and is in the hospital."

Liz looked at me as she spoke.

"He probably had too much to drink."

I didn't want to fight or argue, so I went along with it.

"Probably."

"I'm serious," Liz said.

I merely nodded my head. "Alright. He probably drank too much," I said, hoping that if I just said it aloud, it might feel true. And it made sense. He was at a bar. He passed out. He probably did have too much to drink. But in the back of my head, something kept telling me it wasn't that.

"Let's finish the AP chem lab report," Liz muttered, lifting her folder out of her backpack.

As I gripped a pen, my mom walked into the kitchen.

"Hi, Mom," I said, and she didn't reply.

"Mom?"

"Oh, Ria. Have you seen your father?"

I scoffed. "Do you even know what happened to him?"

She wouldn't look me in the eye.

"Why don't you just call him?" I mumbled.

"He won't answer my calls."

I nodded. "No shit."

Liz kept her eyes on her lab sheet but I watched them flicker between my face and my mom's a couple times.

I couldn't even focus on my mom. I didn't want to focus on her. I wanted to know where Flynn was. I wanted to see him. He was the only one who understood all this. I gripped my phone, texting him.

"You know I found Dad at a bar two weeks ago. He got up and left. I also found him holding my unconscious boyfriend in his lap."

My mom looked at me with confusion.

"Since when did… wait… a boyfriend?"

I rolled my eyes. "You would know if you actually occasionally saw me. Or talked to me. Or asked me normal questions a normal mom does."

My mom's mouth opened, but I wasn't done.

"Instead of having me spend my Friday night running around town looking for your husband." She flinched at the word *husband* and pressed the palms of her hands onto the counter.

"Ria," Liz started. I almost forgot she was here. I watched her walk down the hall, mouthing the words 'text me,' and she stepped out.

My mom didn't utter a word. Her eyes turned red. She struggled to hide the tears tripping over her lashes.

"Fuck this," I mumbled, putting my books into my bag. And then my phone rang and I swear my heart almost stopped.

Flynn: I'm fine.

Fine? I wait two weeks to get a fine?

I glanced at my mom to see her grabbing a trashcan and puking into it. And for a couple minutes, all my rage, all the anger, the red I saw, vanished. And I walked up to her, and wrapped my arms around her waist.

"Mom, what is happening?"

She sniffled and turned to face me, her eyes were dark red and she was repeatedly wiping at her mouth.

"Stomach virus," she told me.

Bullshit, I thought. I didn't know what I expected her to say when I asked, but not a stomach virus. She was too sad for it to be the flu or something. I walked into the hallway, aimlessly typing at my phone and called Flynn.

He picked up on the first ring.

"Hey—" I breathed, and he cut me off.

"Meet me at the back of Linda's diner in 10. Don't be late," he muttered, before ending the call without another word.

Chapter Sixteen

I used to go to Linda's Diner every weekend with Dad. In fact, I don't even know what happened to that tradition. We just stopped going one day. One day's excuse turned into a weekly excuse, and then we just stopped going altogether.

I drove down the old street, my mind wandered from my mom, my dad, and then always managed to land back on Flynn. I wanted to be mad at him. I wanted to yell at him for almost dying, and then leaving me wondering for two weeks if he was even okay. But the second I saw him, even from the back, and even from a distance, it was the same feeling I got when Mom was throwing up.

I just couldn't feel mad, no matter how hard I tried, and how hard I wanted to. I ran up to him, instantly snaking my arms around him from behind, causing him to tremble. I stepped back. Afraid of his shaking touch. What did I do? My eyes moved up his arm, it was so red and so purple. *What happened?*

I remember he walked me to his car, and then he was suddenly winding his arms around my neck and quickly crashing his lips to mine. I didn't bother to push him away. Even when he bit my lower lip, and pulled me flush against him, so quickly and so hard, it almost hurt.

Even when his fingers slipped under my shirt, tracing patterns under my crop tank; because it felt *nice*. It felt good to feel wanted by someone else, and I never wanted the numbing feeling to leave me, so I let him do it all because it had felt like so long since he last touched me. But, I wanted an explanation, I wanted to know why he was gone for those two weeks and why his lip was busted, and why his eyes were constantly red and watery.

The question I always ask myself is, why didn't I ask all these questions? I knew things were happening. I knew certain things were wrong. But I never asked. I was too scared for the answers.

I let him pepper a series of kisses down my neck, and I let him pull my shirt over my head until we were naked from the waist up. I looked at the small purple and red marks on his shoulders. He tried to cover them up. But I saw them.

I flinched at his touch, but he kept mumbling words like "You're the prettiest girl I've seen," and my dumbass fell for all of it. So, when the last item of clothing was off, I didn't stop what I knew was going to happen, rather I weaved his hand through mine and let it go his way.

* * *

I didn't know how I expected to feel after that. Was I supposed to feel like someone else? People always talk about how sex can change you, but I felt no different. Just sore. And stupid. I had always dreamed of having sex with someone I loved, and not necessarily in the backseat of someone's car. But I didn't want to show Flynn that. His fingers were clawing through my hair. He was doing everything the way they do in the movies, and I should have loved it and him all for it. But love just doesn't work like that. Love isn't just forced.

I lifted my head off his chest, leaning backwards to face him.

"Where did you go?" I mumbled, my voice raspy. I yanked my top over my head as he lifted himself up, rubbing at his eyes.

"Can we not talk about this right now?"

I wanted to fight and ask, then *when*? Because that's what I would have done with anyone else. But I didn't, because it was Flynn, a guy who actually liked me, and I was in no position to pass that up. Maybe with time. I pressed my eyes together, and leaned back on him—our breaths the only sound I could hear. *All I need is time.*

* * *

"You did what?" Liz practically screamed at the cafe. I practically had to fly across the table to cover her mouth from screaming any more words. I could feel a blush paint my cheeks.

I shrugged.

"I didn't just expect it to happen, you know. I went to go hear what he was gonna say about him being go—"

Liz cut me off with a grin. "But your mouth just happened to land elsewhere, huh?"

My cheeks burned.

"Shut up."

"What happened after?"

"I just sorta laid there. And then he drove me home," I mumbled.

Liz grinned and I slapped her shoulder.

"Damn, just three weeks ago you hadn't even kissed a boy! Look at you now." Liz's lips pulled into a large grin, and I remember my entire face dancing with smiles and turning a bright red. But for some reason, it didn't matter how happy I could be feeling, that even though I wanted my mind on one thing, it seemed to take me everywhere else.

"I just wish he trusted me enough to tell me what was going on," I mumbled, bringing my glass to my lips.

"It might not have anything to do with trust. He could maybe be embarrassed."

"Of what?" I asked.

Liz shrugged. "You two are really different, yet really alike. From the ways I've seen it, he maybe got high on something, maybe he overdosed, who knows, maybe he just doesn't want you to see the bad parts."

I looked out the window. "I should be able to see all parts. I just wanna know him. I feel like I don't know anything about him."

"He'll tell you when he wants to," Liz told me.

There was nothing else I could have said. I guess I just felt so weird, kissing a guy, having him sleepover at my place, when I didn't know him as well as I wanted to.

And then my phone rang.

FLYNN: Where are you right now?

I grinned.

ME: Stellas cafe with Liz.

FLYNN: Hmm, I'm coming to save you.

ME: Liz is wonderful company.

FLYNN: None better than me.

My lips grew into a smile and I saw Liz throw me a look.

"Ditching me?" she asked.

I rolled my eyes.

"Not yet."

"So he texted?" she asked.

I grinned.

"It's okay, I'm letting this slide 'cause I'm sure I was the same way with Jon."

I laughed.

She was even worse with Jon.

"Remember the day you tried to confess to him? We literally went to his house."

I turned to face her. "Where does Jon live?"

"Is that it?" I pointed at the house we were driving near, and she quickly nodded her head. There was no doubt his family was well played, and as I looked at Liz, her face broke into a smile.

"You're saying I should just ask him to the bonfire?"
(Um yea, what else should you do.)
I said: "Aha."
She said: Huh. (a few seconds ran by) Okay.
I said: So, go.
She said: Fine.

Liz trudged up Jon's narrow driveway, consistently glancing back at me with a nervous look. I let out a few laughs, urging her to continue walking until she reached his front step.

I watched her take in a breath, and then she curled her hands into fists and knocked on the door. Not pounded, or banged. But, she simply tapped. I hauled in a sigh. Her fingers were shaking, her face bright red as she waited for the door to open. After a few seconds, the door briskly opened, revealing, who seemed to be, Jon's sister. Her hair was a fluffy mess, her eyes a light blue. She was dressed in a summer tank top, and white girl shorts as she examined Liz's face.

She smirked.

I lifted my head from the window and stared at the back of Liz's sunny hair. Her hands were tumbling as she peered down the house door. I stood up, deciding if I should not or should step out of the car. The girl leaned against the doorframe, her auburn hair falling past her shoulders. She was petite, her eyes trained on Liz's face, but I could not read it. Her makeup was smeared, mascara under her eyelids and her eyeliner covered half of her eyes.

Oh God, I pressed my fingers to my temple. This can't be happening. But Liz didn't know it. I sucked in a harsh breath and started walking up the driveway, and that was when the girl started speaking. Her voice was sending chills across my spine, and my heart rate accelerated as I watched it all crumble, like rocks falling from a cliff one by one.

"Who are you?" she asked, crossing her flaky arms across her chest. (Like she had one.) Liz stumbled, and then quickly steadied herself, meeting the confused gaze of the young girl.

"I'm here to talk to, ummm, Jon," Liz said firmly, and I wished no more than anything in that moment, than to drag her out of that girl's face.

The girl turned around, calling for someone, and a few seconds later, Jon stood by her side. In seconds, I knew Liz had figured it out. Dressed in plaid boxers, and a white shirt that looked as if he just slipped it on.

Her face broke.

Pieces tumbling.

"Oh God. Liz, come on," I whispered as I walked up his steps. Jon slid his arm around the girl's waist bringing her close, and Liz looked away, cheeks red and eyes blue.

As she turned around, she quickly met my gaze, and that was when I saw two tears trailing down her cheek. With the flick of a finger, she wiped them off and faced Jon with a small smile.

"Hum, never mind. Wrong house," she quietly muttered. Jon looked at Liz, and for a brief second, Liz stared back.

Then, she walked down the steps, once more, breaking down. The door closed, and Liz's pace quickened.

"He's a jerk. Ignore it. It's okay," I said, my voice soft.

"I really liked him," she cried, throwing her hands in the car as she entered her car.

Liz imitated herself. "I really liked him!!!"

I laughed.

"Your poor heart."

Liz scoffed, "Please, I wasn't *that* distraught." I raised my brow.

"Shut up." Liz covered her face. Her fingers wrapped around the glass.

"I will throw this at you."

I lowered my gaze at the latte. "It's too pretty to be thrown at me."

Liz leaned across the table.

"Guess who's behind you."

Before I knew it, I was almost dragged out of the cafe and frantically yelling bye to Liz who was laughing her ass off, and suddenly, I was sitting in his car and driving off.

* * *

Chapter Seventeen

His arm was draped across my seat, and for a good 10 minutes, at least, he didn't say a word. He would simply grin every now and then.

"Where are we going?" I asked. Instead of responding, his fingers drew circles on my bare shoulders. I didn't say anything after that. He kept driving. And he kept drawing circles on my hands and shoulders.

"Just away," he finally mumbled.

I didn't question him further. I simply grabbed his hand. I watched his eyes skitter towards our interlocked hands and a small smile crawled up his lips before he turned back to the road.

I laughed, but it came out breathlessly, like I had been laughing for the past 20 minutes and I was out of breath, but it was just because of *him.*

His grip around my hand grew tighter.

"When I was 6, my mom moved out," he started.

"Maybe she was kicked out. I don't know."

"What do you mean?" I asked.

He sighed.

"I mean, my dad won't tell me. I always told myself my parents were just fighting the way all parents do, and maybe they just, I don't know, divorced and she moved out."

"But—"

"I think he kicked her out." His hands grew red. Warmer.

"Don't worry about your mom, you've done well without her," I told him.

He scoffed, "Have I?"

I turned to face him, my finger sliding across his cheeks. "Shut up."

"I'm serious."

I sighed. "So am I. You're amazing."

"You're just saying this 'cause you're my girlfriend."

My face broke into a grin. *Girlfriend.*

"No, I'm saying it 'cause it's true. You're amazing. You make me so insanely happy, and that means you're amazing. I just, I don't want to hear you talk bad about yourself. It does you no good."

"Ria, you don't even—" He paused his sentence, and now I know he was just trying to say I was saying complete bullshit because I didn't even know him. Maybe if I did, he would have never tried to kill himself. Maybe he would be better. Okay, even.

Too many maybes. I need to stop using that awful word. Maybe was used too much.

That night was one of the most normal nights we had together. One of those that made us feel like a completely normal couple. Picnics by a lake, and hiking and singing, and him holding me close against tree bark, something that made us feel real.

"Should I even bother asking where we're going?" I said with a grin never leaving my face.

"Nah."

I settled with that. I wanted to ask him more, there was always so much I wanted to know.

"So tell me," I started. "What do you wanna do with your life?"

I should have noticed the way something moved in his eyes, but I didn't.

He coughed. And then smiled. And he didn't respond for a bit, instead he snaked his fingers with mine.

"Writer. It's a way for me to, I don't know, express myself in other ways I guess."

"A writer," I repeated, a smile growing on my lips.

"I don't have the grades for anything else."

I sighed.

"But you love it. You don't seem like you would love being a doctor or lawyer or shit. You like writing and people do good with the things they like," I told him.

He released a short sigh, like he had heard those words so many times before and they were just *other* words sliding off some random person's tongue.

"I mean it," I kept going.

He shook his head.

"What about you?"

I swallowed. "Nursing. I want to go to NYUS nursing program." He gently tightened his grip on my hands and my gaze immediately skittered towards them. My eyes were locked on them and I didn't want to look away.

I loved it. The feeling he gave me. Feeling wanted. Loved. Beautiful. It's all I ever wanted, but given to me in a completely, utterly wrong way.

Flynn parked the car near an empty park, with only just the black sky dotted with stars that made the corners of my lips curl into a smile. I wanted to freeze it. I wanted to pause it.

"You're a traditional guy aren't you?" I teased him, my hands pointing in front of us.

He scoffed, "Anything but traditional. Don't let the park fool you."

I nodded my head jokingly.

"Who said we're even eating here?"

"Guide the way," I said.

As we were walking, we were getting farther and farther from the actual park, the benches, and playground.

I wanted to ask him where we were going, but I knew I would get a shush as my response. So I only gripped his hand harder and let him take me where he wanted to go.

"We're behind a house," he finally said.

"Are we going to your h—"

"No. We're... he paused. "Not." He finished coldly.

Flynn turned around in two seconds, his eyes had fallen.

"I didn't mean it like that—" He angrily pushed his face into his hands.

"Hey it's fine, you didn't even say anything wrong. Don't worry about it."

"It didn't matter what I said. It was the way I said it." He just seemed so mad at himself, and all I could think of doing was slipping my arms around his shoulders and pulling him inward, but I didn't, at first.

"You don't need to tell me anything now," I told him, even though I really did want to know everything.

"Really?" *No.*

"Yes, really."

Not knowing was the reason for it all.

He sighed with relief, but I could only smile. All of a sudden, he ran across a field, with me grinning and laughing and chasing after him while running in circles. Flynn took his bag and lifted out a blanket where he set it on the grass. His eyes were glistening. His fingers wrapped around a laptop and he yanked it out and played it on the blanket.

"Your pick," Flynn said shyly, with his eyes focused on the laptop.

"You're adorable," I said, smiling as I bent down on the blanket. And then I started to hear something. Someone yelling. Screaming for someone. It didn't feel real, it was too quiet. I looked back at Flynn to see him frozen and his eyes screwed shut.

"Flynn?" I asked him. He didn't reply.

The voice stopped and that second, Flynn's eyes flew open.

"Should I ask?" I asked him.

"I was thinking," he told me.

I raised a brow. "Thinking?" I shook my head, continuing. "I thought we had a conversation about lying, mister."

The corners of his lips started to lift upwards into a smile.

"You know it's okay to show…" I paused for a second. "Show feelings." I gripped his hand because they were trembling.

"You don't have to act like you're so alone all the time. You have me."

That wasn't enough for you was it?

"Do I?"

I threw my head back, laughing. "Since that day in the car."

"Really? I thought you hated me. You looked so mad at me. And I thought, what had I even done to get this girl to dislike me after 2 seconds."

I thought for a bit. "That was a rough night. I was drunk. On my period."

Flynn never said anything to that. Instead, he turned his computer on. His jaw tightened.

"What's wrong?"

Flynn never responded. I turned to face him, but he wouldn't meet my gaze, instead, kept it focused on the laptop.

"What movie?"

"Your pick," he muttered.

"So you respond now," I teased, but he didn't say anything.

"Flynn, Jeez. What i—" He turned towards me and his eyes raked across my face as his fingers slipped behind my neck and his lips met mine, and suddenly, all my thoughts and questions disappeared.

Chapter Eighteen

"Honestly, screw APUSH. Mrs. Norman just sucks," I muttered, slamming my locker.

"You're just mad you got an A-."

"Screw you."

Liz laughed before turning to face me.

"Your mom's been calling me," Liz blurted out.

"What?"

Liz sighed.

"Like, she's been texting me and calling me. I picked up once."

"What's she even saying? She's crazy," I mumbled.

"She's your mom," Liz said.

I laughed. "My mom?"

"Yea, she gave birth to you."

I shook my head.

Liz shot me a glare. "So what, you're adopted?"

I breathed out.

"She's not my mom in a different sense. Look, cool she called you, but I don't car—" Liz rolled her eyes before gripping my shoulders.

"She's worried about you."

"Um she can talk to me if she is. Which, she never does," I said, trying not to feel frustrated. My jaw was starting to clench. Who the fuck does she think she is? Worried about me?

She's never bothered asking me anything. She's never even *home.*

Liz's face collapsed, in the sense she had a void of any emotion, and her eyes softened. I hated that look.

"I'm going to math," I said quietly.

"Please, don't tell her yet!" I turned around and I felt a scratch run down my back, and my neck, and my face.

Mom? What was *she* doing here?

And there she stood, more like hunched over near the trashcan. Her face had turned pale and her eyes would glance away from mine. I didn't even want to look at her. I wanted to run up, and scream at her face, and hug her, all at the same time. I hated how I could feel two completely different emotions all at once.

"Liz, what the fuck is she do—"

"I'm so sorry," Liz started mumbling, walking towards the end of the hallway.

What was going on? Liz had never looked so guilty. She couldn't even look at me.

I threw my hands in the air as my face turned redder with each passing second.

"Can someone tell me what's going on?"

My mom walked towards me. Thank God the bell already rang and classes were in session.

"I didn't want to tell you this at school," she started, her voice growing quiet.

My fingers found my backpack strap and I started to twirl it around my finger.

"Tell me what?" I said swallowing. Her eyes were skittering all over the place and never landing on my face.

She choked back on a sob. "I'm so sorry," she started. "I'm so terribly sorry," She kept mumbling.

Fuck.

"Mom, for what?" I asked her, my voice barely audible.

She lifted her head up and stared straight past me. She didn't respond.

"Sorry for *what,* Mom?" I asked more firmly this time, my hands started to curl into fists.

When I looked up, tears were crawling down her face.

"I'm pregnant," she finally said. And in that second, tears blurred my sight and I was crying before my mind even processed what it was she said. It was like her sight alone was enough to make me feel like this, and then I was falling into the wall, sobbing.

"You're, *what?*" I whispered.

She placed a hand over her belly, smiling sadly.

"I'm pregnant."

I shook my head.

"With Dad's baby, right? *Dad's baby, right?*"

"Mom, it's MY sibling, right? Then, then that's amaz—" I kept hysterically mumbling, words were slipping off my tongue like vomit. I knew I sounded crazy. I was praying it wasn't what I thought it was. I was praying she wasn't who I thought she was. I wanted her to prove me wrong. But she didn't.

"It's—" she choked. "Not your father's."

My father's?

"What the fuck?" I started, my hands wrapping around my head.

"You cheated on Dad?" I was saying this for myself. I didn't want her to answer it. I already knew what the answer was. I knew it the whole time.

"You had sex with someone who wasn't your fucking husband and… and now you're pregnant?"

My mom didn't answer.

"That's why you would throw up. It's all making sense now, *oh my God.*" I thought Mom maybe had an eating disorder. But no. She was pregnant.

"Ria—" she started. I walked towards the exit door.

"Don't call me that." My teeth were clenched and my hands were running through my bag to find my phone so I could call Flynn.

I walked outside. I didn't even want to look at her. Is it bad I expected it? I knew one of them was cheating. I gave Dad so much shit for something he never did.

"I'm still trying to make this all work, Ria."

She was running out towards me.

"Where are you going?" she asked, still crying. I turned around.

"Why the hell are YOU crying? God, poor Dad," I said.

"You think I wanted this to happen, I—" I cut her off because I couldn't hear her anymore.

"Mom, it takes two to fucking tango," I said sarcastically, as my head shook back and forth like I was confused. But I had never understood something so well.

I started walking down the sidewalk with no idea of where I was going. I just needed to leave.

"Ria, please don't leave. Please. Where are you goin—"

"Anywhere you're not."

ME: Flynn pick me up

Flynn: Look up ;)

I didn't spare a glance behind me before rushing towards his car and yanking the door open.

* * *

"What happened?" He asked me.

I shook my head. I thought if I kept pretending I never heard that, that maybe it just never happened. I stayed silent for a bit.

"Do you have that E on you?" I suddenly blurted, and he turned towards me to look at me as if I was crazy.

"Ria…" he started, eyeing me carefully.

"You asked me a couple days ago, I said no. Well now I'm saying yes."

"Flynn. I want it," I said again, more firmly this time.

He sighed, pulling out the pills from a small bottle.

"Not yet, not here."

I groaned.

"Jesus, Ria."

"I don't need to explain myself." Flynn's arms snaked around my waist.

"Whatever you want," Flynn muttered, his grip on the wheel growing tighter as he drove.

I nodded my head.

"What even happened?"

I didn't move my eyes from the window.

"My mom's pregnant," I said.

"Is that a bad thing?"

"It is when the baby's dad isn't mine," I mumbled.

"Wait *what*?"

I sighed.

"My mom—"

"Cheated on your dad," Flynn finished, his eyes softening.

I scoffed, "Don't give me that look."

"I'm giving you no look."

I turned away. I didn't want him to look at me like he was sorry for me. Nothing even happened.

"That sad look, I hate it."

Flynn rolled his eyes.

"What? Do you want me to grin at you?" And in that second, I didn't want to talk anymore. I didn't want to think about what happened at school. I didn't want to think about what Liz knew. I didn't want to think about my mom or dad or even Elaine. Just Flynn. Just what was happening right in that instant. *Just wanted to think in the now.*

So, before my mind forced me to stop, I slipped my hands around his neck and yanked him towards me, just as his lips crashed into mine. His hands sifted through my locks as mine snaked around his waist in an effort to be pressed flush against him. He pushed me into the car seat as his fingers gripped the bottom of my tee shirt and glazed across the skin above my hip.

"What are you doing?" he mumbled against my lips as I lifted his shirt off.

"Shut up," I mumbled, before pressing my lips on his again. I could feel his smile.

"Wait, Ria—" Flynn pulled away and I noticed something running in his eyes. My fingers slipped around the hem of his white tee and I used it to cover my chest.

I rolled my eyes. "You're stopping *now*?"

The corner of his lips turned into a smirk. "You can wait a *second*."

I frowned when he started driving again. I slipped his tee shirt over my head.

"Where the hell are we going?"

"A park," he said. I turned to stare at him, my cheeks instantly heating up at the fact he wasn't wearing a shirt.

His eyes glazed across my face at a red light.

"Nice shirt," Flynn said with a small smirk fitting his lips.

I swatted his shoulder.

"Shut up. It was easier to put on then mine."

"You can just admit you like it."

"Shut up again."

My phone rang. I glanced down to see it was my mom. I didn't spare it a look longer than two seconds before angrily stuffing it into my pocket.

"Your mom again?" Flynn asked with a sigh.

I just nodded.

"Why don't you pick up? She's worried."

I scoffed, "She's just scared I'm going to tell my dad. I'm 100% sure my dad has no idea."

"Are you going to say anything?"

I lowered my eyes at my hands as my voice turned soft and quiet.

"It's not my thing to tell. My mom needs to tell him." I shut my eyes, lowering the window.

"Poor man. He's going to be the last to know," Flynn mumbled.

I kept my eyes closed.

"I know." I could feel tears brimming the corner of my eyes and I stuffed my head into the corner of the seat.

"I was so bitchy to him."

"You didn't know, Ria."

"I never know anything in this damn family."

"Should I drop you home?" My eyes opened instantly and I turned towards him.

"No no, please. Please, *no*." I couldn't go there. I didn't want to go there.

"I want it," I told him, hoping he would understand what I meant without having to actually say it.

"E?"

I nodded.

Flynn chuckled, his laugh cutting right through me.

"Ria, 10 seconds ago you were practically sleeping."

"Yea, that was *10 seconds ago*."

"I don't kno—"

"Please. Just this once."

Flynn didn't respond but, instead, turned the car on and started driving.

* * *

Chapter Nineteen

"Has the girl never been high before?"

I couldn't feel *anything.* I felt light and heavy at the same time, and I loved it all. I leaned into the couch, a grin on my face as my eyes began to close. I could hear the distant ringing of my cell phone. But I didn't bother to move to see who was calling.

"Ria." I blinked twice. And in front of me, only mere inches from my face, was Flynn.

"I really like this couch," I mumbled. My fingers gripped one of the pillows and I put it on my stomach. "It's a nice couch," I said.

Flynn released a breathless laugh.

"A nice couch?"

I nodded, smiling.

"Mhhhhhhhhhm. Can we take it home?"

"I think that's where we should take you, babe."

"Babbbbbeeeeeeee. Say it again," I said with closed eyes, feeling a smile grow across my lips. Flynn didn't say anything for a bit, until I felt his breath at the shell of my ear, and he softly uttered, "Babe."

I stuffed my face into the pillow.

"I wuvvvv that."

"God, I am never letting you get like this again."

I giggled. "I… um…" I couldn't even form a coherent sentence.

"Ria, you can't even talk."

I lifted my finger in the air. "I am talking nooowwwwwwww."

Flynn shook his head but couldn't help the grin that spread to his face, his eyes, and everything in between.

"I can't believe you like me," I blurted.

"How could I not?"

I looked away.

"I feel I'm not someone you would typically date."

Flynn sighed.

"So?"

"Why?" I started my sentence but a yawn took over.

"Why what?"

"Why do you like me?"

Flynn's eyes bored into mine and I swallowed. His gaze didn't leave mine.

"There doesn't need to be any reason *why* I like you, Ria. All that matters is I do."

I could feel my heart practically fall into my stomach. I leaned over, snaked my arms around his waist and placed my head in the crook of his neck. It was one of those small memories that I look back at and cry. I cry because I lost that chance. I can't put my head in his neck like that anymore. He can't whisper in my ear that he loves me, but it doesn't matter, because he never did. Neither of us knew what the word meant. I still don't.

****

"Riiiiiiiiiiiiiiia." My eyes burst open to see Jon in front of me. My head is throbbing and I feel puke rising up my throat. Little pieces from last new flew into my head. But it was like a blurry picture, where you can make out the important parts but none of the details.

I remember *him.* I remember the feeling I had when I was with him. I remember the pills. I remember crying. And then laughing. And then doing both.

"Ria, what the fuck happened?" Jon asked me, sitting on the edge of the bed. I wrapped one arm around my head, sucking in a long breath. I couldn't say. I didn't want to say. I didn't want it to be true.

"Is Liz here?" I asked, ignoring his question.

Jon's gaze averted to the ground.

"She was. She left when you woke up," he said.

"Didn't want to see me, did she?" I mumbled, pulling one of the blankets off me and sitting up.

Jon exhaled.

"She knew, Jon, that Mom was…" I paused, my voice almost inaudible. "Pregnant. The whole time. And she didn't even bother telling me."

"She was told not to tell, Ria. Look, it's not her thing to tell. Your mom had to be the one to tell you."

I sighed, pressing fingers to my head.

"I don't care, Jon. She should have told me my mom was fucking pregnant. Maybe it would have saved me the embarrassment of finding out at school."

"Talk to her."

I nodded my head. She's been my best friend for too many years to count. I can't even be truly mad at her if I tried. Jon threw me a pair of new clothes and left me to change as I tried to process everything that had happened in the last 24 hours. I slipped Jon's sister's shirt over my head, and pulled her shorts up my legs before leaving the room.

"Hey, Jon?" I called as I walked down the hallway.

I saw his mom at the bottom of the stairs. I started to smile.

"Ria! Sweetie, breakfast is at the table." I was worried Jon might have dropped hints of what happened last night, I didn't want to look bad in her eyes.

"Oh gosh, thank you, Mrs. Merrick!" I said as the corners of my lips lifted up into a smile and I hopped down the stairs. She walked into her office and closed the door behind her. Jon's mom was a lawyer, but she worked from home. It was nice Jon was able to see her whenever he wanted. Sometimes I wish my mom was like that. She used to be. And then some wheel's tires flattened in her head.

"Your mom is actually the cutest human being," I said, sitting on the table. Jon rolled his eyes.

"You don't live with her."

I laughed, chugging orange juice down.

"Oh, your phone is there. I think your sister's been calling," Jon said and I immediately stood up and practically ran to the counter. *12 missed calls. 9 messages.*

ELAINE: I don't understand
ELAINE: Ria, pick up!
ELAINE: I don't want to be alone tonight. Dad's not here.
ELAINE: YOU HAVE A PHONE FOR A REASON.
ELAINE: Mom's having a baby, what the actual fuck?
ELAINE: Pls.
ELAINE: I give up with this whole family.
ELAINE: Mom's a whore. Dad's a weak child.
ELAINE: Fuck this.

Oh God. My fingers move as quickly as they could to call her. It rang and rang and rang and then went to voicemail. I wanted to slam my fist on Jon's counter.

"Fuck," I mumbled before trying to call her again, but it went straight to voicemail. I didn't see Elaine until two days later.

Chapter Twenty

This day was the first time I noticed, I guess, how human Flynn was. How much he was like everyone else. And how much I painted a picture of someone who was only in my head. I wasn't with him. I went to his school to surprise him. After he brought me those gifts at school, I thought I could give him something in return. He hadn't been picking up his calls—he seemed to be awful at that lately.

I gave up trying to contact him through any type of technology. So I thought, why not just visit him at school?

I parked the car outside of his school's campus. I went around asking people if they had seen him, and people all gave me different answers. I ended up walking all around the inside of his school. I even found his locker; it had FLYNN in large letters and it was plastered with pictures of Flynn playing basketball. He looked so young in the pictures.

"This guy played basketball?" I asked a girl whose locker was next to him. I had no idea he even played a sport. She eyed the picture like she hadn't seen it before, which I found strange since she was his locker buddy.

"You didn't know? He was like varsity team captain last year. He just stopped playing. Apparently he got some job that was like really important," she said, shrugging.

"He quit a sport which he was captain of… for a job?" I repeated, completely astonished.

"*Apparently*," the girl said, grabbing her books and stuffing them in her backpack.

"Have you seen him?" I asked.

"Not since 4th period."

I nodded my head as I mumbled a timid thanks and walked down the hallway. Kids exited the school. At this point, most of the buses had already come and the parking lots were practically empty.

And then I heard it. It was faint and didn't sound real. I saw Flynn bent on the ground with his back against the wall, and his head stuffed into his hands as his body shook with sobs. I swallowed, my fingers losing grip of my bag strap as it dropped to the ground.

"Flynn?" I whispered, but my voice was leaving me. He didn't move. I crouched on the ground beside him. I could see the tears sliding down his cheek. I gripped his hand. He didn't flinch. He didn't lift his head up. Instead, he gently placed his head on my shoulder blade and I wrapped my arms around him.

"Flynn, what happened?" He never answered. But a couple seconds passed by and suddenly he stood up, wiped at his eyes, and the tears that looked like they had stained his face had vanished, and he *looked* completely and utterly fine. Like what happened five minutes ago never happened.

"It's okay to feel, you know," I said quietly. He wouldn't look at me.

"Bad grade. Just, you know, worried about college." But his eyes were all over the place.

I shook my head.

"I know when you're lying. Don't even try," I mumbled.

"Ria, I really am just stressed about college. You'll get it next year."

"Flynn."

"*Ria.*"

"It's just school." I stared at him with intent. The way he cried, the way his body was trembling beside mine, it didn't seem like school related stress.

"I wish you would just tell me."

Flynn sighed.

"It really is. I got a D on a paper and it dropped my grade in history to a C. Just scared I won't get in anywhere," he muttered sadly, and I moved in towards him and engulfed him in a hug.

"You have time to bring it up. You can always take a gap year, don't even stress about history. Your major is English."

"One month. I know," he said.

"That's better than no time."

"I know bu—"

"No buts." I grinned as he swiftly pecked my cheek.

"Are you okay now?" I asked him.

He merely looked back.

"I will be, if we get yogurt." He grinned sheepishly.

"You played basketball?" I blurted. His eyes grew.

"I did."

"You stopped?"

Flynn sighed. "That's why I used the word *did*, Ria."

I didn't want to say anything after that. I could already feel the tension growing and I hated the silence that drifted between us, so I started walking. I remember after that, Flynn walked to a WALGREENS saying he needed to pick up medication from the pharmacy. Five minutes later, he walked out with flowers and a grin dancing across his face.

"I lied," he said, when he walked into the car.

I laughed, and reached forward toward the flowers.

"Why?"

Flynn shrugged. "Doesn't have to be a why. I wanted to."

I grinned, my fingers instantly looping around his.

"I felt bad. About before," he finally said.

"It's okay, Flynn. You didn't do anything wrong, I just hope you're feeling better. These flowers are stunning." Flynn turned to glance at me, a smirk playing on his lips.

"Sounds like you're talking about the girl sitting next to me." I rolled my eyes, my fingers glazing across the baby-pink petals.

"Ria, I really like you," Flynn said.

I laughed. "I like you too."

Flynn shook his head.

"Don't say too. Makes me feel like it's not true. I like you more than I like myself. I like you so much that I get scared to think about what might happen next week, or next month, or next year. I can't stop thinking about everything after all this right now."

"I can't either," I said, when truth was, I hadn't even thought about anything ahead of everything at that moment.

"But that's not something we can change or fix," I said.

He shook his head.

"The worst part of it all…" he paused, glancing at me with a sad smile. "Is we're the only ones to have control over everything *after*."

"Flynn—" I started quietly. "Ria, you don't understand… there—" I cut him off, almost pleading.

"Then let me. Tell me things. Fill me in on your life. Flynn, I didn't know you played basketball, and I know that's not something that's even a big deal, but I just…" I breathed out. "Just wanna know things. I wanna know *you*."

"I love that," he admitted.

"Love what?"

"That you want to know. No one ever tries."

"Am I everyone?"

Flynn looked at me before squeezing my hand.

"Fucking bless, you're not."

"I like you being curious. People always make curiosity seem like something so bad. It makes it look like you just, I don't know, care."

I grinned, leaning my head against his shoulder. Moments like those felt everlasting. They felt like a forever. Like they were on a record player that never stopped spinning. It felt like when I read a book that completely took me over, where even when THE END was written, it never really felt completed. It never felt like *the end.*

For those next few weeks, I would come home to randomly placed napkins with little facts about him. I never realized how he got in the house until Elaine blurted she would let him in. I kept them in a wooden box under my bed, just for myself to read whenever I wanted to.

When I was 8, I broke my leg from sitting on a grocery cart with my dad, and I made him move it faster and faster and then... whoops!

Pickles are my favorite. After you, of course.

I never learned how to tie shoes.

When I eat Oreos, I never eat them individually. I pile them on each other and swirl whip cream at the top. I eat them like a cake.

I steal napkins from cafes. Just for this very reason.

I only eat the green skittles. They're sour and bright. Reminds me of something like life.

I used to sleep with my eyes open.

And I love a girl named Ria.

One night, I was reading them and my mom abruptly walked into my room. She couldn't even get a word out of her mouth because her body was trembling.

"Mom?"

"I did it. I finally did it."

I didn't want to even ask her what she meant. She continued speaking, her words flying out like word vomit.

"I drove him away. I broke it," she mumbled, leaning against my wall with her eyes focused on the ground.

"Broke what?" I felt a lodge grow in my throat. I didn't want her to say it. I didn't want to hear it.

"This *family.* He's gone." And that's when my hands started shaking and my head started spinning, with all my thoughts crashing against each other, not letting me form a cogent thought.

"Where's Elaine?" I whispered, because my voice felt *gone.*

"I don't know. I can't tell her yet, Ria, please."

"You're a bitch. I don't even want to look at you."

"Ria—"

My hands curled into fists. Her face turned pale when she realized.

"Elaine was right," I started. "You're a whore. You weren't faithful to Dad who loved you. And you, what, threw it all away for some one-night stand?"

My mom couldn't say anything. Or maybe she could but she knew better then to speak.

"Where's Elaine?" I repeated.

"She left."

"And you don't care? What the fuck?"

I walked out of the room, letting my mom cry, and saw that both of the cars were gone. I called Elaine and she never answered.

"Liz, he—"

"Ria, oh my God, I'm so sorry for not telling you. I should have. I was just scare—"

I shook my head, even though she couldn't see me. I should have never been angry with her in the first place.

"Liz, its fine. It was something my mom had to tell me, not you. Honestly, don't worry about it."

"Thank God."

I laughed into the line.

"Slight problem, though. I need your car."

"I'm at your service," Liz said before ending the call, and I exited the garage and walked up the hallway to see Mom looking at herself in the mirror. I didn't let her see me. She was staring at her stomach, her hand gliding across it with the smallest smile tickling her lips.

I wanted to scream at her. But I couldn't help but smile because I might have a sister or a brother. I didn't even take a second to look at it like that, and maybe something good can come out of something that seems utterly terrible. I leaned against the wall until Liz texted me saying she was in front of my house.

"Mom," I interrupted her and stepped in the room. She removed her hands in an instant and quickly wiped her eyes.

"We're going on a hunt for Elaine. Come on."

* * *

Chapter Twenty-One

Me–Flynn: You're home, right?
MESSAGE READ FOUR HOURS AGO

I sighed, turning off my phone as Liz drove us out of the neighborhood.

"Ria, I didn't know—" my mom started, but I did not want us to fight with Liz in the car.

"Save it," I mumbled, turning around and leaning my head against the seat. Liz glanced at me, her eyes dropping, and my heart felt like it was falling into my stomach.

"Where could she be?" Liz asked me.

I had no idea where Elaine was. I figured she was with Brian. But this felt different. It didn't feel like when she *normally* just left the house. This time she was trying to make a statement. Prove her point. She knew this was coming; she knew something like this was running in the family. My mom remained quiet the whole drive and it scared me how calm she was, like she had no care in the world.

I turned around to look at her.

"How do you do it?" I blurted.

She blinked twice.

"Do what?"

"Act like nothing's wrong with anything."

"Ria, just because I l*ook* like I don't feel anything doesn't mean I don't."

"Your daughter's missing."

"She isn't missing, Ria. She needed to just breathe. Forget for a bit." *It didn't feel like she was referring to Elaine.*

I threw my hands in the air.

"How are you so...?"

"Ria, stop," Liz finally said, her voice so hard to hear over my mom's screaming.

"I'm sorry, it's just—"

Liz shook her head, smiling sadly.

"It's not that. I just don't want you to say something you're going to end up regretting."

I squinted at her.

"What do you mean?"

"She is your mom after all."

I sighed.

"I know Liz, doesn't mean I can't be mad at her. My family is practically gone because of her." I lowered my voice because I didn't want mom to hear every little word I was uttering.

"I know but—"

I shook my head. "Let's not talk about this, right now we need to find Elaine."

"Where do we even go?"

I lowered the window on my side, pushing my head forward.

"Just keep driving. The town is small. She's somewhere."

We ended up driving for over three hours that night, before finding Elaine at her elementary school park, just sitting and swinging on one of the swings. She didn't notice we were there. I just stood and watched her for a bit, the way her hands continued to grip the chains tighter with each passing second.

I told Mom to stay in the car and Liz to make sure she didn't run off towards Elaine.

I wondered why she came there. At first, it made no sense. I figured she would be at a bar, or a party, the way she was the night I met Flynn. But this was different. *Sh*e was different. After a couple minutes, I snaked my arms around one of the swing poles and stood there silently until she noticed.

"Ria…" Her eyes went wide and, in seconds, the swing had come to a complete halt. I didn't ask her why she was there. I didn't tell her to never do that again. I didn't question anything. I simply gripped her waist, looping my arms around her waist, and yanked her into a long hug, one that I never wanted to let go from.

And then I heard some mumbling, talking, but so quietly I couldn't make out the voice it belonged too. Elaine turned stiff.

"Who is that?" she whispered. There were two people sitting on benches at the end of the park.

I squinted.

"I can't tell. The hoods cover their faces." Mom came running down the sidewalk and Elaine turned around.

"Mom," I started.

She shook her head.

"Can I just talk to her?"

I didn't say anything. I turned around to look back at the benches to see if those people were still there but they were gone. Liz was already half way up the hill.

"Liz!" I called when she reached the benches. I stopped moving up. She bent down, her hands sifting in the grass. She stayed bent down for so long until I saw her fingers curl around something, and she stood up, her eyes bright and wide.

"Ria."

"It's fucking drugs."

"They were dealing?"

Liz didn't say anything. She eyed the small bag.

"Liz, put that back down," I told her.

"What are they?" she asked. I didn't want to tell her they were E. I didn't want to explain to her how I knew. I didn't want to tell her Flynn gave me E more than once.

Instead, I shrugged and skittered my gaze back at Mom and Elaine.

Liz dropped the bag in the grass and quickly ran down the hill. I remember feeling sick to my stomach. I remember trying to think *who* would do that. I remember trying not to think that the truth was, well, true.

I was last to get in the car. I offered to drive but Mom insisted, her face lit with a grin that I just wanted to wipe off her face. I didn't say a word in the car. I ignored Flynn's texts. I ignored Mom's voice. I just tuned it all out. Liz's gaze skittered across my face, never leaving, but I turned to face the window so no one could see the tears roll down my cheeks.

At first, I didn't even understand why I was crying. My head was so clogged, I couldn't even find the reason. And then I realized, in this car was my new family, and one person was missing from it, someone who might never want to see me again. When we got home, I didn't even say bye to Liz or wait for my mom or sister to walk in with me, I just ran up to my room. Above my desk, was a string with 17 pictures to represent me being 17. Four of the pictures were with Dad. I untied the string and rolled the four pictures down, slowly gazing at each one as they landed in the palm of my hand.

Without really thinking, my fingers wrapped around a pair of scissors, and I cut out Dad's face in all four of the pictures, and threw his face in the trashcan. I didn't know what to do after that. I just remember collapsing onto my bed, still in my jeans, and cried until my head just turned everything off.

* * *

When I woke up the next morning, I wasn't feeling that whole school thing. But I went anyways. I just wanted to see him. Have him hold me. I wanted his thumb to glaze back and forth across my hand. I wanted his arms snaked around my shoulders. I wanted to taste his smile. I wanted to see his eyes glisten when he talked about writing. I just wanted *him.* I didn't want to annoy Liz with bringing him up, so I refrained from even telling her I was leaving school.

I ran out the main doors, telling the office I wasn't feeling well, and they let me go without a word. I could already feel a smile poking at the corner of my lips as I let my bag plop into the passenger seat and I started the car.

I remember I always just wanted to please him, make him grin, laugh, the deep one he always does, and just make him feel alright. I didn't want to fight. I didn't want to disagree. I didn't want any complications. But the fact I didn't want any, only made us have more. Because relationships aren't supposed to be perfect. They're supposed to have cuts and holes and that's what makes them beautiful; because trying to make a relationship *work,* is what makes it beautiful. I was trying to make something that wasn't supposed to be. I was trying to make something work for two people who didn't know what they wanted.

That day, I stopped to get Flynn yogurt.

"Thank you!" I said after paying.

"Your dress is so cute and yea, anytime," the cashier had said with a smile, and I grinned back, mumbling a shy thank you before running to the car.

When I arrived at his school, I was hoping he was still eating lunch. I gazed down two halls and the large lunchroom, but I never saw him. My stomach tumbled.

"Hey, do you know a Flynn?" I asked, realizing I didn't even know his last name. *His girlfriend doesn't know his last name. Nice.*

"A Flynn?" *Okay, why are the people all bitches at this school.* A girl, slightly taller than me with red hair and a septum pricing that I hated I loved on her, towered in front of me.

"Yes."

"Maybe. Why?" she mumbled, her eyes focused on my face.

"He's a…" I paused. She raised her brow. "Friend. He's a friend and I brought him a gift."

"Awww, did you ditch school to bring him a love letter?"

I could feel my cheeks heating up.

"Do you know where he is or not?"

She scoffed, "If you knew him at all, you would know school's not his thing."

My voice was starting to turn quiet. It was the way she said everything. Like she knew him better than himself.

"School isn't anyone's thing," I said.

She rolled her eyes.

"He never shows up. Sometimes he says he's sick. Sometimes he claims he felt no need to come to school. Sometimes he just doesn't come because he doesn't want to."

I sighed.

"Do you know where he—"

"Lives? No, I don't. We never fucked in his house." Her lips curled upwards into the smallest of smirks before she unlocked the code into her locker. *Was it bad I really didn't care?* Like her words didn't pick at anything with me. They didn't make me feel warm and heavy. They didn't make me feel like slapping the girl. It just slid right past me. That should have been a sign.

Instead, I gave the girl the sweetest smile I could muster in the moment and sauntered down the hallway. By this point, the yogurt had already melted, so I sat on the curb in the parking lot eating the rest of it.

I had taken the bus here and didn't want to take it back home, so I called Liz.

"Hey, Liz, I'm so sorry to ask you this, but could you pick me up after school from the hospital on 25th?"

She laughed into the line. "Ria, what are you doing at the hospital?"

My cheeks burned and I praised the lord we weren't facetiming right now.

"I had to give the hospital some of my mom's forms for her pregnancy," I mumbled, even though I had no idea what I said, it kinda made some sense.

"Oh, oh, oh. Yea, I'll come right after school."

"I love you. Seriously."

I could feel her grinning.

"Oh, I know."

"Okay, shut up, Liz," I said with fake exasperation before ending the call and walking towards the hospital.

I didn't want her to know I ditched school for a guy who wasn't even *at* his school since he constantly ditches his.

There were only 30 minutes until school was out, so I just roamed the trails behind the hospital. I checked my phone to see if Flynn had called, but he hadn't. I tried again. No response. I didn't know why I carried it on for so long. He was there one day and then gone for three days, and then he would come back as if he never left. But he *would* leave for days. Without a trace or text or call. He was just *gone.* Always was.

I waited for Liz, but when it reached 4, I decided to call her.

She picked up on the last ring. There was no sound on the end of the line. I could just hear her breathing fast and heavy, like she had been crying.

"Liz?"

"I saw Jon, holding that girl's hand, and she had her head on his shoulder, and fuck me, Ria, because I started crying and I broke it off with him. I couldn't stand watching them together. He knew I was standing there. I just—" her voice had gotten soft and I could tell she was trying hard not to cry.

"I'm coming over," I said into the line.

"Ria, I'm so so sore…"

"You have nothing to apologize for. I'll uber to your place, okay? Go downstairs and make some tea, and watch a movie until I get there."

* * *

I ran into Liz's house and knowing her, the front door would probably be unlocked. I slipped inside and immediately threw my shoes on the ground.

"Liz?" She didn't reply to me but I saw her watching TV on the couch, with ice cream and a blanket. My lips quirked into a small smile at the site of her doing exactly what I said.

"Babbbbbbbe," I murmured softly, and she glanced up as I slid beside her and gripped her hand.

"Are you sure you really broke up with him? Liz, you two were forever. Are you sure you sa—"

She threw her head back and laughed, but it wasn't supposed to be funny.

"Um yes, Ria, I saw. I don't know, I mean, they're friends. But the way she clings to him pisses me off. And I got a C on my research paper, so maybe I was just in a bad mood. I should call him, right?" I smiled.

"Hell yes, he's probably dying."

Liz sniffled but a smile grew on her lips. She walked out of the room and I sat on her couch, just as my phone rang; a text from Flynn.

My heart felt like it was swallowed and then puked out.

Flynn: I'm sorry, will call you in two days.

Two days?

What the fuck?

I pressed his number but it kept ringing and ringing. *This doesn't make sense.*

Just as I was about to call or text him again, Liz walked into the room with a grin filling her whole face. I laughed.

"Guessing it's all good now?"

She nodded her head.

"I think. I really don't want us to ever, like, leave each other. I really like him, I can't see myself with anyone else, which scares me, because he could just stop feeling things for me." Liz looks at the ground. I release a short breath, walking towards her.

"Liz, if he does stop liking you, which I'm sure he won't, then you'll know he wasn't the one for you, because he doesn't want to be with you. Right now, he does. Worry about now."

"How's your mom?"

I shrugged. I hated how I felt my stomach just tumble at the mere mention of her name.

"Fine, I guess. I don't really know. I haven't, like, sat down and talked with her about everything that's happened."

Liz planted herself on an island stool.

"You plan too, right?"

I released a short breath.

"I guess," I mumbled, unsurely. "Because I didn't know. I wanted to talk to her about it, but it didn't seem like she wanted to explain it all to me. I just never understood. I didn't get why she would leave Dad like that. I guess that, love, feeling eventually leaves."

Chapter Twenty-Two

That weekend, I stayed home and studied for SAT's. My test was in three weeks and I needed the 1,500. Elaine had been gone for most of the weekend and had been blocking my calls, so I figured she was with Brian. Was it bad I wished Flynn would be with me all the time, the way Brian was with Elaine? I wish he didn't just vanish for three days and come back as if he never left at all. I wish he acted normal. I guess that's what I wanted. I wanted a simple, normal boyfriend who went and got me flowers and took me on movie dates every Friday.

I didn't want to leave the house, mostly because I wanted to wait until Flynn called me, so I just stayed cramped at the dining table, surrounded with books and food. *I missed him. I wanted him. I needed to see him.*

I started to think I was crazy because I was obsessed. But part of me just loved it. Loved liking someone. Or so I thought it was a like. I didn't realize I was so *obsessed* with the idea of someone loving me, that I created someone in my head who didn't exist.

Me: Liz. Study break?

LIZ: Oh shit, yes, pls!!!!! I'm gonna bang my head in a wall if i stare at the word sat one more time

Me: Same. pick u up in 4

When I picked her up, the first thing she did was run up to me and swung her arms around my neck, and pulled me into a hug.

"I love you. Have I ever said that?"

I laughed into her neck.

"Oh, Liz. What happened?"

"I'm, like, really good with Jon now, and I just was a mess, and you helped. I love you."

"I've always wanted to be a godmother, so I needed to make sure you two turn out alright." A giggle escaped Liz's lips before redness spread across her cheeks and she glanced behind her.

She lowered her voice.

"We haven't, you know, done…" Her voice turned quiet. "*It.*"

I shrugged. "It's no biggie. Whenever you want."

"Have you talked to your mom?" Liz asked as we walked into the car. I sighed out of exasperation before slowly turning my head to face her.

"Why do you keep asking?"

Liz's gaze fell to the ground as she gripped the handle of the car.

"I don't know," she murmured. "I just feel like part of it is my fault, so I just, I don't know, want to make sure you two are okay, I guess."

"It's not your fault, Liz. It's he—"

She cut me off. "It's everyone's. It's your mom's, it's also your dad's, and it's the guy who had sex with your mom's fault. You can't just blame it all on her you know."

"I know. I'm not. I can't help feeling mad when I see her though. I know she's not the only one to blame, and I know there are, like, so many truths to what happened, and I just don't care about it anymore. The only thing that's on my mind is my dad. And if he's okay or not."

"I think he knew," Liz said, her words barely audible, as if they weren't even said. I started the car.

"I think so too." I believed it as I uttered it. I figured he did. It must have been obvious to him.

"God, I don't even want to imagine how and what he feels right now, like, fuck." I pressed my forehead to the wheel. Liza hands sifted through my hair as I sighed.

"Let's just get out of here."

"Best thing I've heard all week," I mumbled as the smallest smile tingled on my lips, and I drove us out of the neighborhood.

"I was thinking the park," I blurted.

Liz stared at me skeptically.

"The park?" Her brows furrowed in confusion, and I slowly nodded my head.

"I just... I want..." I wasn't able to string a coherent sentence.

Liz laughed.

"Park we go. I'll push you on the swings."

"Last time you did that, I fell off, like, 7 feet in the air," I mumbled with a small laugh.

"You're so light!"

"That is no excuse. Remember, I broke my wrist."

Liz rolled her eyes. "How could I? You brought it up for those next two months. Guilt tripped me into doing anything for you."

My lips quirked into a smirk.

"You're an asshole," Liz said with a grin.

"Yettttt..."

"Yet I adore you and your stupid ass."

I grinned to see Liz shaking her head beside me and rolling the windows down as the wind filled our faces.

"My hair!" I groaned, attempting to press the button on to roll the windows up.

"Is messy anyways," Liz finished with a smirk, and I wanted to push her out the door.

"Little fucker you are."

"Ria, turn! You're gonna miss it." Liz's hands waved all over the place, just as I turned my blinker on and turned into the parking lot of the park. For some reason, I could already feel my heart hammering hard in my chest and my breaths quickening.

"You almost missed it." Liz rolled her eyes as she stepped out of the car.

"Exactly. Almost."

That day, we pretended like we were five. We went on the playground. I slid down the slide. I even climbed up it. We swung on the swings together. I let my hands fly in the air and let my hair dance along with the wind. It made me miss my childhood, and all I had were small memories that made no sense. It made me miss Dad, lifting me up in the air so I could play on the monkey bars because I was never tall enough. But he helped. He always helped.

Maybe I just wanted them to get a divorce. I always wanted something to end the fighting between them, and a divorce would make that possible.

It wasn't like I wanted them to split, I just wanted the fighting to be over. I guess Dad leaving was that. That was the end to the one in the morning yells, and the sudden vanishes to the bar, and the midnight run around towns trying to locate my dad. I knew they loved each other. We all knew that.

But they had their cuts the way that every relationship has. Some can be stitched and some just bleed.

I tightly gripped the swing before I caught sight of the place where me and Flynn ate once. It feels like a forever ago when it was just last week. God. I missed him. I didn't know you were capable of missing someone, so much where even thinking about them makes my stomach tumble and tumble.

I let go of the chains and lightly jumped off the swings. I saw Liz sauntering off into the grass so I ran up to her.

"Liz where are you going?"

"The bathrooms! And no, I'm not fucking peeing in the porta-potty over there. I will walk the mile to the bathroom." I released a small chuckle before patting on her shoulder.

"Good, you finally get a work out in."

She threw me a glare and continued walking.

I walked towards the spot I ate with Flynn, near the big tree. In the distance, I could see the old house, and I remember the way Flynn reacted to it. His eyes turning sharp and his face fell apart into little pieces that couldn't be pieced together. I don't think they still are.

I kept walking closer until I was directly in front of it. I could make out small hushed voices and there was a car. I didn't know what I was thinking—wait, I really wasn't in the first place.

I just had an unexplained urge to go closer. Like it was some haunted house and I wanted to explore it. It was old, and the white paint was basically coming off. The door was half open but the corner of it had fallen off its screw. The stairs leading up to the door were crooked, and the handles were collapsed on the ground beside each step. It didn't seem too inviting.

I stopped as I reached the driveway and, just then, the voices lowered and became too soft and barely audible for me to make out who it was talking.

I crept to the right side of the small house, and I remember seeing Flynn and Elaine, mumbling to each other. He was wearing a dark hoodie, the hood of it covering his face. They hadn't realized I was there yet, and I wasn't ready to ask him what the fuck my sister was doing.

That hoodie. The same one the night we found Elaine in the playground.

And that was when a rushed gasp escaped my lips, and it was too loud to be hidden.

Elaine was the first to turn around. Flynn faced the other way, but I already knew it was him. She quickly pushed her hands into her dress pockets before her eyes grew as she looked at me.

"Ri... Riiiii-a?" she stuttered, and her cheeks instantly went red.

"What the fuck?" I couldn't say anything else because I had never been more confused in my life.

"Wait, Elaine, what are you doing here with... with him?"

"I didn't come here to secretly make out; work him or something," she mumbled, unable to meet my eyes.

"Don't joke about that."

"Don''t worry, Ria, he's yours."

"Elaine, what are you doing here?"

She didn't respond. Flynn still hadn't uttered a word or even turned around.

"Flynn, I know it's you." His body stiffened, as he slowly turned around but wouldn't lift up his face.

"What's that in your pocket?" I asked him, even though I wasn't that clueless or naive to know that it was drugs.

"Which one this time? E? O? Oxycodon? Maybe even heroin."

"He was not giving me fucking heroin."

I EYED Elaine.

"A drug is a drug, Elaine. What did he give you?"

"E. He gave me E." She lowered her gaze to the ground, her feet moving together, as they did when she felt ashamed.

"Why the hell would you need E?"

"I don't need anything, I wanted it."

"You know these things can eventually turn into needs."

"I'm not stupid. I just wanted it once."

"I can't believe you. I know Mom and Dad's thing was messing with you, but resorting to drugs—"

"Don't fucking act like you didn't either. When you found Mom was pregnant, you went and got high with him. I'm not a child anymore. I want to forget. I don't want to think. I don't want to remember any of these things. I don't care if it's not permanent, I can deal with it later. I want to forget it now. I don't want to think right now."

I didn't have anything to say. Part of me was embarrassed Flynn told her I practically begged him to give me E that night. I'm trying to be mad at Flynn for giving the drugs, but for some reason, I can't find it in me to be mad. I'm so insanely happy to see him that none of what's going on is even registering.

"Flynn?" I breathed. "Why would you tell her? Were you trying to convince her into—"

"He told me because I asked," Elaine blurted.

I turned to Elaine.

"Please, Elaine. Think about this. Getting high is fun in the mome—"

"That's all I care about. Whatever happens after, I can deal with. I want something to help me right now."

I shook my head sadly.

"It doesn't help."

"It makes you feel other things and I don't mind feeling anything else. As long as it's not what I feel right now."

My lips were pressed into a firm line as I looked her in the eyes, to see them only black.

"Elaine," I started, softly but she cut me off only shaking her head.

"Just this once, Ria."

I shook my head.

"Isn't that what you said when you came with us to the bar that night?"

Elaine didn't respond. She merely kept walking away, her shoulders punched mine as she strutted off.

I glanced up to see Flynn with his gaze still on the ground as I walked towards him, his body began to move and his eyes bored into mine. I hadn't seen him in what felt like months but was only a mere week.

"Where... I just... I missed you." I couldn't even bring myself to talk about what the fuck he just did, selling drugs to my sister. But seeing him made me forget about all those things.

Flynn pulled his hoodie off, a small smile making its way towards his lips.

"I missed you too. So much, you have no idea."

"Where have you even been?"

Flynn sighed.

"I've been at home. Helping my dad." One thing I will never get over was how fantastic of a liar Flynn was. I walked closer to him until our noses were only a few inches apart, and if I moved a centimeter, I could press my lips to his.

"I missed you," I repeated.

"Course you did."

I swatted him.

"Shut up."

I wanted to bring up the drugs. I wanted to ask if this is a thing he does. I wanted to ask if that was him at the park.

But I didn't ask anything. I didn't push. I pretended what I saw with him and my sister never happened. I pretended he hadn't done anything.

Because pretending was as easy as breathing.

My hands curled through his hair as his hands weaved around my waist, and his other grazed the open skin near my belly button.

I found myself falling into him, but just as I was close to collapsing on his chest, his fingers swept under my chin and his lips met mine, and I forgot about everything.

His kisses made my legs shake. His kisses made my heart drum in my chest, faster than I thought it was capable. His kisses made me feel everything I ever wanted to.

So I snaked my arms around his neck and yanked him closer, tilting my head to the side to deepen the kiss as I threaded my fingers through his hair. My back was pressed to the side of the house as Flynn's body was crushed against mine. His hands glazed under my top and his quick fingers moved to my back.

"No, not here," I breathed against his lips, clinging to him.

His fingers gripped my bra strap.

"Why not Ria?"

"People. And outside. And—" my sentences weren't making sense.

"You're not making sense." Flynn laughed and I turned away.

"Well, you do that to me." I could feel my cheeks heating up and I wished I wasn't so close to him.

"Oh yea?" He grinned. "What do I do?"

"Make me nervous and make me say stuff I wouldn't normally say, and do stuff I wouldn't normally do. And you just confuse me, because sometimes, you're all I see in my head, and I don't even know if that's mentally okay. You're all I ever think of," I breathed out, averting my eyes from his face, until his finger slipped under my chin and forced my eyes to meet his.

"I love you."

I closed my eyes because none of this felt real. I poked his nose.

"What are you doing?" he asked me with a smile, and I let out a short laugh.

"Just making sure you're real."

Chapter Twenty-Three

I told myself not to push it. I told myself not to ask him about anything that just happened, because I knew I wouldn't get the truth I wanted anyways. Not the complete one.

I knew it was wrong to not even ask about the drugs. I knew it was wrong to not question him as to where he was the past few days. I knew it was wrong to stay silent. But It was like my voice was gone and the words simply stung my tongue.

Instead, I kept my arms wrapped around his waist. I pressed my cheek to his chest, and drowned in the tranquility of just his heartbeat.

"Liz." I murmured against his chest, my eyes closed like I was asleep.

"Crap, she's waiting for me."

Flynn chuckled, his hands tugging at my ends, and I smiled quickly, releasing my hands from his waist and stuffing them into my pocket.

"Will you call this time?" I asked him.

"I'm sorry, babe, I should have told you that I couldn't talk earlier and not a day ago."

"Maybe you should have told me why you couldn't talk in the first place," I mumbled, but I meant it to only be heard by myself.

"I really just wasn't feeling well. I needed a break…"

"From me too?"

"Ria—" he started.

"No, hey, your health is more important. I'll call you tomorrow, okay?"

He could only nod his head as I swiftly pressed my lips to his cheek, my touch lingering longer than needed, but I didn't want to move away. I never wanted to.

"You better answer," I said.

He turned on his heel and left me with a wink.

I ran up the hill and back to the main park. I saw Liz, fallen asleep against the tree and I laughed out loud.

"Liz! Liz!" I yelled, before turning towards her. Her head started to shake as a yawn escaped her lips and her hands started dancing in the air.

"Where the fuck have you been? I spent like 10 MUNITES looking for you before…" she scratched her head, confusion running across her face.

"I slept. This is a good napping tree. Also, where were you?"

"I'll tell you in the car," I said.

* * *

"I… I saw Flynn and Elaine talking," I said. I couldn't bring myself to talk about the drugs. I was embarrassed.

"Okay?"

"That's all," I muttered, facing the window.

"Ria, what the hell was your sister doing with your boyfriend at that creepy ass house?"

I shrugged.

"Ria, seriously, that's just strange. He wouldn't talk to you, and then you find him with your sister, and he didn't even tell you what was going on?"

"I don't trust him," she finished, and this time, my head snapped.

"You don't know him! He's not normally like that—"

"Ria, you don't know this kid either. I know you try to pretend you do, but you don't. Now tell me what the fuck they were doing, because there's no way you didn't make him tell you what was going on."

I sighed, my eyes skittering from the road to the brake. I could feel my fingers start to tremble against the wheel because I did not want her to know.

"They were only talking," I said quietly, glancing away so she couldn't look at my face.

"They were doing something, Ria. No way after all that you didn't force him to tell you something."

"It's none of your business, all I came to tell you was where I went. I don't know what they were doing." My tone was turning sharp, and my grip on the wheel was only growing tighter as my fingers turned red.

"I don't like him. I don't know him and you don't either. You don't know what you're doing!"

I bit my tongue.

"He just goes off for days at a time and you let him come back with no explanation. You're okay with him not telling you anything. Why? That makes no sense. You're okay with not knowing? You just want to stay in the dark and date a guy who you claim you know but, Ria, I bet we both know this kid the same and I'm rarely with him."

"Wow." I couldn't say anything else.

"You know what I think? I think that was Flynn the night at the park. I think he drug deals for money because his dad lost his job and can't work—"

"Stop." I couldn't let her talk more. I couldn't hear it.

"How do you know about his dad?"

Liz rolled her eyes. "You told me."

"Liz, stop. You can't just throw around the fact he sells drugs."

"It's true isn't it? I saw the way your face changed when you saw the bag at the park that night we went looking for Elaine, and when you saw those people leave on the hill. Ria, I'm your best friend and I'm not stupid. Let me guess. He was giving some drug to Elaine, because Elaine needs a distraction from what's going on with your parents and she decided drugs were the way to go. And he needs the money. So, it doesn't matter who he deals with as long as he gets the cash in return," Liz finished and I ate a lump in my throat.

As a job? He always had E on him, and maybe that's what he meant by helping his dad, by trying to get money so he can go to college. And what he meant by he wasn't good at anything, he couldn't get a job, so he resorted to this.

"Oh God," I muttered, my heart sank into my stomach and I felt like puking.

"He sold drugs to your sister. And you still want to be with him?"

"I just…" I breathed out. "I like him."

"He's a drug dealer, Ria. You're so blinded, this is insane."

"Maybe this is all he could do, okay! He just needs a little help and I'm not going to stop being with him over one thing —"

"One *big* thing," Liz grumbled.

"You're supposed to be on my side. You're supposed to agree with me and help me, and not just yell at me like you're my mom." I sighed, pinching my nose.

"Ria, I am. But I just think this is so sketchy. I want you to be careful and actually ask him this time what the fuck is going on, because you need to know. *You need to know who you're dating,*" she finished quietly.

"I'm going to walk home," I murmured.

"What?"

I turned to Liz, repeating my words more firmly.

"I will walk home because I need a therapeutic walk."

"Ria—" she began, and I shook my head as I gripped the car handle and pushed it open.

* * *

My hands were curled into fists the whole walk home. The worst part was, I agreed with everything she said and I hated myself for it. I didn't even try hard to ask him where he was or if anything he was even telling me was true. I never try hard enough.

All I wanted was to see him, and when I did, it was like everything I wanted to ask disappeared and I could only focus on *him.*

Me to Flynn: Is this, like, a thing you do?

He replied in less than a minute.

Flynn: What?

Me: Selling drugs.

Flynn: What are you trying to say?

Me: Do you, like, deal?

I saw the three little bubbles show up, and then they vanished.

Flynn: Just a couple times.

I left him on read because I didn't know what to say after that.

Flynn: Ria, it's hard, okay? Your sister begged me and I couldn't say no, because she kept pushing and pushing and she just looked distraught.

Me: Drugs won't help.

Flynn: They helped you that night.

I turned my phone off just as it beeped again.

Flynn: I'm sorry, okay? It was a one-time thing. It won't happen again and I'll never give them to your sister again.

Me: What if she comes to you distraught and begs? You gave in last time.

Flynn: I won't, I promise.

Me: Don't use that word.

Flynn: I'm sorry, babe): I couldn't go to school, and then my phone broke so I couldn't even explain.

Me: You were taking care of your dad. right?

Flynn: Yea, he was being weird with the medications and I needed to stay with him.

I sighed. I hated how I couldn't even feel that mad. I just felt my stomach lightly flip every time he looked at me, texted me, and touched me.

Me: I'll see you later this week :)

Flynn: I love you.

Me: I love you more.

I ended up walking around my house for another hour, just aimlessly roaming around and taking in the heat, and the brief wind that hit my hair ever couple minutes. I was walking down my block and I saw another car in my driveway.

I remember running down the block with my heart rapidly drumming in my chest because I thought it was Dad. And my whole face glowed with smiles until I stepped inside the door, and the second I heard the voice talking, I knew it wasn't him,

At that point, I wasn't in the mood to speak to anyone. Whoever it was, couldn't get my mom to stop laughing like she was 14, and I hadn't seen her grin like that since her anniversary with Dad. I quietly slipped upstairs and collapsed on my bed, shutting my eyes in seconds.

* * *

When I woke up, I could still hear his voice downstairs. I wanted to eat something, so I knew I would have to go down there anyways. As I walked down the hall, I passed Elaine's room to see her sound asleep on her bed. She was still wearing her converses. A small smile grew on my lips as I walked towards her and quietly untied the laces and yanked her shoes off her feet. I grabbed a blanket and laid it across her body as she shifted a bit, and I used that as my chance to run.

"Ria?" my mom called out for me as I was walking down the stairs.

I stepped into the kitchen and across the island was Mom, and on the other side, was a man I had never seen before. The second I eyed him, my mom's cheeks turned bright red.

"You must be the oldest! Your mom would not stop talking about you." The guy grinned, holding his hand out. *So he knew me.* And he was a guy who couldn't get my mom to stop turning red. I knew who he was but I couldn't believe it. I hadn't been thinking about what happened for a bit, and now it was all hitting me like a wave.

"Yea, nice to meet you. What's your name?" I asked, trying to keep my voice as still and calm as possible, but inside, I was fighting to *scream.*

He glanced at my mom, his eyes saying, *'Did you not tell her?'* I ignored the look, plastering a smile across my face.

"I'm Jace. Your mother's… uh…" He cleared his throat as my gaze skittered between the two.

"Friend?" I offered, because I knew by that point who he was, but I knew he couldn't refer to himself as the boyfriend yet.

"That's one word." He laughed, but I didn't find it funny. My mom's face fell a bit before she started talking. Her hand was pressed on her stomach and I swallowed.

"Ria, Jace is…"

"The baby's dad," I finished quietly as I stared at the ground. "I figured. I mean, you wouldn't stop giggling and you were turning red every second. Mom, can I talk to you for a second?" I mumbled, trying hard not to look at Jace at all.

We went into the bathroom.

"Mom, what is going on?"

She sighed.

"I wanted you to meet him, you and Elaine. I wanted us all to, maybe, have dinner—" I cut her off.

"Fuck no, not yet. *Can you even let us breathe?* Do you not know how hard Dad leaving was on Elaine? We barely just found out you were pregnant, and you already want us to meet the dude?"

"Lower your voice," my mom mumbled. "He wanted to meet you two so bad, and I couldn't say no. I couldn't tell him they didn't want to meet you."

"Do you know Elaine's going crazy?"

My mom averted her gaze from my face as she fiddled with her thumbs.

"I like Jace. I like him a lot. He makes me smile and laugh and cry all at the same time. I haven't felt this happy in a long, long time," she finished softly.

I ate the lump in my throat. "But Dad?"

"Baby, I will always love your dad. Always. But it just fell apart a long time ago, and we tried to make it work, but forcing something doesn't work."

Forcing something doesn't work. I remember thinking it's like if Mom and Dad didn't love me, I just wanted someone to take their place and hold me close and hug me, where they stuff their head into the crook of my neck, and steal glances and kisses from me. I just wanted someone to love and love me back.

I couldn't hear anything related to this anymore.

"Can I have dinner? I'll be quick and then leave you guys to it."

My mom shook her head.

"No, no, eat dinner and talk to him, he really is nice—"

"He's not Dad," I finished, anger seeping into my voice.

My mom didn't respond for a second and she sadly shook her head at me.

"Of course, he's not. Your dad's *Harry* and this is *Jace*. And Jace won't ever be your dad, and you can choose to think of him however you want, but he's staying," my mom muttered before opening the bathroom door and walking back to the kitchen. I remained still for a bit before sighing and following in my mom's steps.

"I think she wants to go to NYU." I heard my mom telling Jace as I walked into the kitchen, forcing the smallest smile on my lips. Jace raised his eyebrow.

"NYU huh? I went there for graduate school. Really fun school and fun city." I nodded my head.

"You're a junior?"

"Yea, I'll be applying in a bit. It's my top choice. That and Fordham."

"If you need any application tips, I can always be of service," he told me, and the corner of my lips curled into a smile.

"That would be nice, thank you," I told him, and he nodded his head as my mom rummaged through the pantry.

"Ria, do you want ravioli?"

I nodded my head.

"So, what do you do?" I asked Jace, suddenly curious to know more about him.

"I'm a paralegal, I work at Rossyes and Lyndermans Law firm in Manhattan," he answered with a grin.

"So where did you and my mom meet?" I asked, finally asking the question I had been dreading, but the only one I really wanted to know.

Jace coughed, and looked away.

"Ria, we met at a bar in the city. She was upset and I was just there, I'm sure you know the rest." I flinched, even though no one touched me. After that, everything was just coming out like word vomit and the words stung my tongue, but I just couldn't stop myself.

"You know my dad?" I started, just as I saw my mom's face collapse in the corner of my eyes.

"You're not him. You can't just waltz in here and pretend all of this is okay, because its fucking not. You ruined our family. You got a married woman pregnant. You can't just be all happy walking in here. My dad's gone because of you. I don't care if you say whatever crap my mom fed you about them already being a mess, it doesn't matter. Those problems were small, my mom having sex and getting pregnant was just the wonderful cherry on top of the ice cream. They could have been fine. My dad could still be here." My voice started to shake. "I just can't handle seeing you replacing him," I finished, and I hated how I could feel tears sting the corner of my eyes.

The strange part was, he didn't seem shocked or surprised at what I said. Like, he expected it to happen. I couldn't move. My feet had stopped functioning. Tears covered my vision and I slowly collapsed onto the ground, stuffing my head between my knees.

I saw Jace get off the island stool and walk towards me.

"I knew this would happen," he sighed.

I watched my mom leave the kitchen.

"What?" I asked, my voice cracking.

"There was no way you could have gotten over your dad leaving so quickly. And I don't mind anything you said. Yea, I was at a club because I lost my job, and your mom was there because she was having a fight with your dad. We got drunk. It happened. Honestly, I don't know what more to tell you or how many times your mom can say sorry. *It happened.*"

I released a breath. My face was still stuffed into my knees.

"I know," I muffled.

"You know?"

"I know what happened," I said quietly. And I did. I got it. I didn't understand it. But I got it.

"I'm sorry for dropping all that on you. And I can't believe I'm even telling you this, of all people, but I just… I miss him," I sighed into my knees.

"Your dad?"

I nodded. His hands wrapped around my shoulders and much to my surprise, I didn't shake them off.

"Of course, you will. And I know I can't replace him whatsoever, but I'm always here. And I'm gonna try to, I guess, just be there. Be a supporter," he told me and I couldn't help but lift my head and smile at him.

"You mean that?"

He nodded. "Of course."

I sighed. "My dad and mom had been having problems for the past two years. He stopped being there, I guess. He was just a mess. And so was my mom. I guess love is just one big mess."

He cocked his head to the side, a grin flashing across his face. "I'm trying to fix that mess." He paused. "I know this seems like it's quick and I really can't help myself. I like your mom, a lot. But I know you kids have gone through a lot with everything with your dad. I'm just gonna back off, in a way, for a bit. Give you guys space. *Let you kids breathe.*" I laughed at the last part. I stuffed my face into the palm of my hands with embarrassment.

"You heard that all didn't you?"

Jace chuckled before standing up.

"The bathroom is right there after all." He pointed at the door directly behind me and I laughed, my cheeks heating up. My mom stepped into the kitchen and Jace walked up to her, pressing his lips to her cheek. I saw the way her whole face broke into a smile, her lips, her eyes, everything. And I couldn't help but smile to see how happy he made her.

"Did Elaine sleep through all that?" Jace asked, and I laughed as I helped my mom make dinner for her and Jace, grinning the whole time.

Chapter Twenty-Four

The rest of the night was spent talking to Jace, who said he could offer me an assistant job at his firm next year. I went to bed just as Jace and my mom went to the movies.

"Elaine?" I called out the following morning, but I was answered with silence. Mom left a note on the kitchen table saying she went to the grocery store. I couldn't find Elaine.

To Elaine: Where you @

Thank God she answered in 3 seconds.

Elaine: With Brian. Don't worry.

I breathed a sigh of relief before putting my phone away in my pocket.

I couldn't stop thinking about the night before with Jace. I felt guilty for liking him so quickly. It was just the things he was saying were things I had always wanted to hear, and when he said them, I just loved it.

I didn't realize the front door was open until Flynn barged into the living room unannounced, and I let out a chilling scream. I couldn't get a word in before he started rambling.

"I'm so-so-so-so-so-so-so-so-so beyond sorry," Flynn said, turning around to close the door behind him.

"I'm a shitty boyfriend. And I can't just say sorry over text for something like that. I know I'm keeping you in the dark. I don't have the best relationship with my dad, okay? And when he wants me to stay home with him and not go to school, I have to. I can't really say no to him or—" Flynn paused, his voice lowering. He never finished that sentence.

"Just like any dad, he would get mad if I didn't listen," He murmured quietly.

"He took my phone and I just couldn't contact you. I should have when I got my phone back." He didn't say anything about the drugs and I didn't even bother asking. I knew he would say the same thing he said before. I latched my arms around his neck and pulled him into a hug, gently pecking his forehead.

"Thank you for that," I smiled, before my lips quirked into a smirk. "But I mean, you could have let me know you were coming. But I'm not complaining over the dramatic entry," I teased as redness crawled around his cheeks and his neck.

"Shut up."

I laughed.

"Really, thanks for telling me all that. Are you and your dad okay?" His eyes wouldn't meet mine after that and he simply shrugged.

"You know how family can get," he muttered with his head down. I swaddled his waist and placed my cheek on his chest to hear his heart beating briskly. I glanced up at his face, my fingers touching his chin.

"Is he still mad?" I asked quietly.

Flynn chuckled. It didn't seem real. I didn't ask. His stomach released a noise, signaling his hunger, so I made a mental note to make him breakfast soon.

"Yea, or he wouldn't let me out of the house." He paused before speaking more. "Who am I kidding anyways? I would leave my house to see whether my dad wanted it or not." I grinned.

"You're so cute," I mumbled into his shirt as my fingers twirled around the collar of his dress shirt.

"And the dress shirt? With the dark wash jeans? Fancy." My fingers started to cloak around his neck, just as he released a guttural groan. My fingers tapped his jaw.

"What's wrong?" I teased, grinning.

"I don't like you just pressed on me like this," his voice was thick as he cleared his throat.

"You don't?" I frowned, jokingly backing up into the wall.

"Hmmmm, guess I just won't get close to you again." I loved being able to make him squirm like that. I heard his stomach grumble again.

"Shut up," he groaned, and I threw my head back, laughing. I gripped his hand, my fingers running up and down his wrist as my other hand slipped under his shirt, tracing patterns across his stomach. I felt him shiver and I glanced up to see his gaze sharpening at me. My hands moved towards his back and I felt him flinch under my touch. I moved back, confused.

"Hey, are y—" I started, quietly because I didn't understand what was going on. He shook his head.

"I'm just cold," Flynn muttered, his voice barely audible. I lowered my hands out of his shirt and I placed them on my sides, suddenly embarrassed.

His stomach made another noise.

"You're hungry," I said.

He shrugged. "I haven't eaten since, like, breakfast yesterday."

My eyes widened. "*What?*"

"It's nothing. I just was, um, busy."

My lips turned into a frown. "Too busy to *eat*?"

"I heard you were stressed about your SAT's," he stated, ignoring my words altogether.

"Yea, super scared. I sighed up for the march one, which gives me like two more weeks. I really need the good score too."

"What was your PSAT score?"

"1,440," I mumbled.

"1,440? Ria, that's amazing! You're nuts to think that's not good."

"What did you get on yours?"

"A 2,150," he said, and my eyes went wide.

"A *2,150?* Flynn, you probably got into some really good schools." He didn't say anything, but I felt his feet shift a bit. His eyes couldn't land on my face as he talked. That's when I realized I hadn't even heard of him talk about college at all.

"Yea, I guess," he uttered. "But, I just wanted to tell you that… that I'm sorry, for never telling you anything."

"I adore you."

He grinned. "You sure?"

I nodded.

"Of course," I murmured, but I wasn't thinking of my words. I was just *saying t*hem.

"Did you tell Liz? Like, where you were?" he asked me.

"I told her a bit," I muttered. Flynn narrowed his eyes at me.

"You're getting weird, did she say something?"

I shrugged.

My voice lowered. "She should just mind her own business."

Flynn raised his brow. "What do you mean?"

I exhaled out of annoyance. "She was just telling me what to do and I don't need that. I get she can think what she wants to think, but she just doesn't get *us*."

A short laugh escaped Flynn's laugh. "Sometimes *I* don't even get us."

He continued, "I'm guessing you shut her up. So, go apologize," he said, and I hated how he just knew everything.

"For what?" I scoffed, even though I did know.

"She gave you her opinion. Just say you're sorry. You need your best friend in this mess called life. It all becomes easier with one," he mumbled.

"Okay…"

"You do. *You need a best friend. You need a best friend.* It's hard without one. And don't just throw them away or fight all the time. *You need a best friend,*" he kept repeating, his voice growing soft.

"Hey, you okay?" I asked, gripping his shoulders.

He cleared his throat just as a smile magically appeared on his mouth.

"I'm just saying to say sorry. That's all."

"Okay." I laughed to lighten the air around us, it felt like lightning was crackling. "I will. You want breakfast?" I asked as I made my way to the kitchen and watched Flynn plant himself on a stool.

"Okay, Chef. Omelet, please."

"As you wish," I beamed, before grabbing a pan and turning the stove on.

* * *

Flynn left a bit after I made him breakfast, just as my mom got home exhausted and immediately fell asleep on the couch.

I wanted to talk to her, hang out, because it seemed we hadn't just sat and really talked, without me yelling at her, in so long.

I texted Liz saying I was coming over, and just as I was walking down the driveway, I felt someone's hand grip the nape of my neck.

"Boo," Charleston whispered into the crest of my ear.

I rapidly turned around.

"Okay, *what the fuck was that*?" I hissed.

Just as his mouth opened, a giggling Elaine walked up the driveway, hand in hand with Brian. I lowered my gaze at their hands and smirked.

"So that's where you were all weekend."

Her eyes twinkled and I laughed.

"Wanna explain what happened?"

Her cheeks warmed up.

"I would, *uh*, rather not." She looked into Charleston's eyes who cleared his throat as Brian ran his hands through his hair, awkwardly glancing at the sky.

"Hmmmmm," I sang, teasing the couple. I turned to Charleston.

"So, you're just third-wheeling?"

"Hey!" He put his hands up in surrender. "They said they were gonna watch all the *Harry Potter* movies. No way I could pass that up. I can handle a lovey-happy couple, don't worry. If I *need* to puke, the bathrooms right next to the TV!"

I ruffled Elaine's hair.

"Alright, have fun. Mom's home though. And that dude Jace might be too, El—"

"I know who he is, Ria. I just won't talk to him. Not yet." She interrupted and I watched her grip grow increasingly tighter on Brian's hand.

I sighed. "Okay, yea, just watch the movies."

As she walked up the stairs towards the front door, she winked. "Oh, *we will*." Charleston and Brian laughed, and I walked into my car, starting it just as I yelled, "Mom's home on the couch. So no funny business, Elaine! Or at least find another make-out spot."

She threw her head back and laughed, and I realized how much she was glowing.

"Does the bedroom work?"

I rolled my window down.

"Oh my fucking God, *Elaine.* Don't leave Charleston out"

He cut me off. "I mean threesomes are a thing, right?"

I pressed my temple to the wheel, gagging.

Elaine squealed. "Gross, Charleston. You guys are like 12."

He shrugged.

I rolled my eyes as I drove out of the driveway and waved my fingers.

"Elaine," I narrowed my eyes, "I mean it. And just help Mom if she needs it."

She nodded her head before eagerly wrapping her arms around Brian's and walking into the house as Charleston followed behind.

"Fucking idiots," I mumbled.

I drove to Liz's apartment and I raced up the stairs, banging on the door.

The door swung open revealing her mom.

"Henrietta, I didn't know you were stopping." I smiled, hugging her.

"I just wanted to see Liz, is she here?"

"Yea, she's with Jon down the hall," she pointed.

I grimaced.

"I can come back lat—"

Just as I was turning on my heel, I could hear Liz running down the hall and I saw her almost slip on the wood.

"Ria!" She threw her hands up before pulling me into a hug.

My lips turned into a small smile as I cleared my throat.

"I just wanted to say I'm sorry for flipping out on you yesterday. I shouldn't have just left." She squeezed my waist, yanking me into a quick hug.

"Hey, it's fine! I am in no place to tell you what to do. As long as you're a smiling doll, I'm content," she beamed. *I am, right? I am happy with him*? I mean, I always need to see him because I always want to, and he makes me feel a million things at once and I loved each one.

"You seem better with your mom," Liz commented, and I nodded my head. I guess so? But still, I see her, and sometimes I think I can only see red everywhere just clouding my vision.

"Yea, for sure," I mumbled. It was partly true. I could never bring myself to tell the whole truth. It was better this way. Like, I didn't want to expose myself to what *I* really thought.

"Elaine mentioned the boyfriend dude, guy," Liz stated with a confused look, and I laughed at her, shaking my head.

"Oh yea, Jace! He's really nice. Way better than I expected. It kinda makes the whole thing better."

"And *Flynn*?" She raised her brow and I could already feel my cheeks warming up at the mere mention of his name. The corner of my mouth curled upwards into a smirk as I started walking and winked over my shoulder.

"Jon!" I yelled, just as the dude crept out of the bathroom.

"You love listening to our talks don't you?" I teasingly crossed my arms over my chest.

"Interesting stuff." He shrugged. I playfully hit his shoulder blade before running into the theater room as I grabbed the remote and started searching through the movies.

"You guys were watching *Arthur*?"

Liz ran into the room.

"Also known as the best show on this earth."

I rolled my eyes.

"My God, you two are such babies."

Jon glanced at Liz with a grin. "I mean, she is my baby anyways." I laughed and sunk into the couch.

"Cute," I murmured. Liz and Jon situated themselves on the end of the couch and picked *Guardians of the Galaxy.* We were, maybe barely, 10 minutes into the film, just as my phone started ringing and I left the room.

"What?" I hissed into the line, trying to keep my voice down.

"Dad's been trying to call you all day, she stated, and I froze, every limb in my body couldn't move. *What?* I didn't think he cared. I didn't think we even mattered considering he walked away without a goodbye. *He didn't fucking say goodbye.*

"What?" I repeated, my breaths slowing down.

"Ria, you blocked him didn't you? That was the dumbest fucking thing to do. He's been freaking out all day and called me, like, four times saying he wants to talk to you."

My voice was caught in my throat.

"*He left.*" It felt strained.

"Ria, call him. He sounded so desperate to talk to you. Like he was crying."

"He left. *He walked away*. Without a word, except a fucking letter."

I could hear Elaine's breaths across the line.

"I know."

"How are you so okay with this?"

"I'm not," she mumbled. "Why do you think I went to Flynn? I'm not. I'm *trying* to be okay with it all. Dad called me and I talked to him. It just… helped." I didn't respond. My head was aching and it just hurt. It all hurt.

"Just call him. Hearing him is nice." The line went dead as I leaned against the wall, thankful the sound system for the movie was loud.

I pressed *favorite*s on my phone contacts. Dad was first. I pushed unblock, biting my lip before holding down the call button.

It rang and rang.

"Ria?" Dad breathed, and I could feel my body just *crumble* because it had felt like an eternity since I heard him.

I swallowed the lodge in my throat. "Hey, Dad."

"You were ignoring me," he stated sadly. I bit my lip harder, feeling blood seep through the cut.

"You left without a word or notice. You literally vanished. I didn't want anything to do with you after that—"

"You can't talk to me like that, Ria, I'm still your dad. I left because I couldn't handle seeing your mom. She told me that Jace kid might move in and I just cracked, okay? I had to leave. And saying goodbye was too hard. I tried calling the next day, but you never answered. I figured your phone broke. And then a week went by. No call. And then another four days and I gave up and called your sister. Blocking me? You th—"

"I did it because I wasn't ready to talk to yet. I was scared and I just didn't know," I interrupted.

"Didn't know what?"

"I didn't understand everything going on. I wanted to figure out Mom and the whole baby thing before talking to you," I finished, hearing Dad sigh.

"I miss you," I blurted, feeling my cheeks heat up. I felt embarrassed.

"I miss all you guys more than you know. I wish I could go home."

"Where are you?" I asked.

"A hotel in Boston."

"Boston?" I said with disbelief.

"Ria, I was so mad I just kept driving. It was my mistake. I should have stayed and tried to figure out a solution with your mom and you guys. I didn't even stop for a minute to think about you guys. I'm just disappointed you tried to cut me off," he sighed, and I felt my heart twist.

"I just… I couldn't—"

He cut me off, "You weren't ever going to call me, were you? You can't just cut your dad out of your life—" My hands turned into white fists and I could feel my cheeks burning.

"Cut you off? Dad, you cut me off *since high school starte*d. We barely talked. You and Mom fought, like, every day. Don't turn this on me."

"Just call me, every day. I miss you girls. I miss your mom," he murmured, and I released a breath I never realized I was holding.

"Dad, come back. At least get an apartment close by. Not in freaking Boston."

"I plan to. I can't stay this long without you kids." I dwelled on the silence that played between us. It wasn't like the weird or awkward silence, it just felt nice knowing my dad was here, safe and on the other line. *Like he was close to me and just… here.*

"How is your mom by the way?"

I grimaced. "She's happy." I didn't want to lie and make something up.

I could feel my dad smiling. "That's all I wanted. If not with me, someone else to get that woman to laugh, since it seemed all I did was make her cry—" *I couldn't handle Dad talking so bad about himself.*

"Dad, you made her happy once, and she was, for so long. You two just… sometimes, it doesn't work out even if you still love her, and I know she will always love you too. You guys were just too different for it to work anymore, and then, Mom just… *cracked*," I said, referring to her running off and having sex with Jace.

"I'll talk to your mom," was all my dad uttered. I figured he didn't want to explain to me his marriage problems, so I quietly said bye and promised I would call him soon. I walked back into the theater room, a small smile lingering on my lips.

* * *

Chapter Twenty-Five

I remember a few weeks after that, I was with Flynn at the park, the place and bench we're always at. He had barely uttered a word since we had gotten there and I was doing AP exam prep.

I nudged his shoulder and he didn't move, and that's when I felt his body start to shake. I remember that day I begged him to tell me what was going on, but the only thing he fed me were lies and snippets of the truth, never the whole.

"I'm stressed about not getting into college," he said, and I wondered how he could say that since it was already march.

"Haven't you heard back from a lot of your schools by now?"

He shrugged, and I watched a tear slip down his cheek.

"Flynn…"

"It's fine," he started chuckling, but it didn't seem right. None of this did.

"You're crying, don't tell me yo—"

"Ria, fucking stop asking me questions," he grumbled, and I snapped, turning away.

"Then don't fucking cry and tell me you're fine. You can't just cry and not expect me to ask what's up when my boyfriend's crying."

He didn't turn around. "Sometimes, have you ever thought you don't need to know everything?"

My eyes went wide. "I don't know *anything.*"

"School's hard, Ria, you'll learn when you have senior year." I rolled my eyes trying to grip his hand, but he wouldn't let me.

"Flynn, you've cried like this before. I've seen you. There's no way that this is all about school—" He interrupted me, swiftly turning around as his eyes bored into mine.

"It fucking can be..." He was raising his voice and I flinched at the voice and tone, and it didn't feel like it was even him talking. I felt his hand slip around the nape of my neck as his eyes dropped to my, lips but I didn't let him kiss me, instead I turned my head.

I stood up as my heart rapidly drummed across my chest.

"You need to calm down. All I asked was what was wrong..."

"Well, I don't have an answer. Everything just sucks," he mumbled, and my heart sank into my stomach.

"Yep, *everything*," I muttered under my breath.

"If you won't tell me, then at least go tell someone else," I mumbled, trying to see if he would figure out what I was trying to say. *He wouldn't talk to me.*

"What are you trying to say?"

I lowered my voice. "You never let me help, and I'm just worried for you, and you scare me when you get like thi—"

"What? Do you think I have problems or something?" His voice had turned increasingly quieter in the last second as he practically sunk into the bench; something in his eyes that I couldn't quite understand.

I sighed. "No, Flynn, all I think is you have too much in your head and you need to spill to someone before you just crack." I wish I paid more attention to what he was saying and the way he said it all. When he referred to himself having problems, I should have dwelled on things more, but I didn't know because I *simply didn't know him.* I gripped his hand, but he flinched under my touch and my face fell.

"Does it make you feel weird now?" I blurted. I was referring to touching him because I noticed the way he squirmed.

"What?"

"Me touching you."

"No, I'm just cold."

I sighed. "That's what you said last time."

"Maybe because its true?"

"You're cold, so I can't touch you?"

"It makes me shiver," he stated firmly, and I eyed his face carefully before releasing a breath and not giving a reply, because I didn't know what to say after that.

Flynn remained silent for a bit, with his face situated between his hands. And then a young kid came up to Flynn, around my age, and he quietly mumbled words in Flynn's ear. Flynn stood up and walked near a tree directly across the bench.

I saw him lift a packet from his pocket, glance around him, and hand it to the kid. The kid handed Flynn money, muttered what seemed to be a thank you, and then ran off in the opposite direction he came. He was giving him drugs and I felt bile in my throat just watching it happen. I felt like ripping my throat out and throwing up, because I couldn't handle watching Flynn do that.

I saw him avert his eyes from my face just as I stood up.

"Done dealing?" I asked him.

He shook his head.

"I don't do it often."

"Twice I've seen, and that's often enough."

"You act like you've never done drugs…"

"I've done it twice and only because you, like, convinced me…"

He frowned. "Don't put this on me. You were begging that one time," he interrupted, and I looked down, my face heating up.

"Why do you do it?" I asked.

He looked surprised by my question.

"I just," he paused, "I have some and I just sell, and I get money for it. There's nothing much to it."

"How do you just have them?"

He let out a breath. "Ria, I got high a lot last year and I just had some. I don't as much anymore, like, rarely, and I thought might as well sell them because there're some really desperate people who will do anything to have some of it."

"So you're a dealer?"

"No, Ria. I'm not, and *stop c*alling me that. Please."

"Okay," I said quietly as the tension between us grew, crackling like lightning. I started to realize a few things that day. *I started to wonder what we were. Why we were us. Why we weren't working. Why I wasn't feeling the whole thing anymore.*

I was thankful my mom texted when she did, because I didn't know how much more silence I could deal with us, especially between us. I didn't like it.

Mom: I'm sick of you never coming home. I never know where you are. I know you're 17, but I want to see you a little bit now. Can you come home? You're always with that guy.

Me: His name's Flynn.

Mom: Come home! Please. Elaine's here too and she's talking to Jace.

Me: I already talked to him.
Mom: Ria, please.
Me: Give me 5 minutes.
I sighed.
Mom: Change of plans. We're meeting at that Italian place.
Me: Which one?
Mom: ...
The bubbles appeared and then disappeared.
Mom: The one Dad always liked.
I turned my phone off.
I wrapped my arms around Flynn's neck.
"My mom wants me home," I murmured into the crook of his neck, inhaling his smell because I loved it.
He turned around, confusion in his eyes.
"Is she okay?"
"She wants me to have dinner with her and Jace. At Dad's favorite place. She could have picked *anywhere*."
"Ria, your dad isn't dead."
I frowned. "I know. But he's still gone."
Flynn drank in the site of my face, before gently pecking my cheek and walking towards the playground. I remember watching him walk away like it was the last time I was seeing him for a while.

* * *

I arrived at the Italian Restaurant, The Elephant Place, just after our set reservations. I had only gone there with Dad and it felt strange walking in without him, and even more strange to eat without him there. But part of me knew Flynn was right.

My dad *wasn't* dead. It wasn't like I was never going to see him again. He was just temporarily gone. Not permanently.

I saw my mom, Elaine, and Jace, at a booth in the corner of the restaurant, and just as I made my way there, Mom started frantically waving her hands in the air as if I couldn't see her.

I dropped my bag on the floor and planted myself beside Elaine, who was giving everyone that one smile that really isn't one. Mom hadn't said a word to me because she was too busy laughing with Jace and sinking into his shoulder.

"What is going on?" I murmured into Elaine's ear. She shrugged.

"They've been like this all night."

"Hey, Henrietta!" Jace finally said.

"Just call me Ria."

"How was your date?"

I could feel my cheeks burning, a smile growing on my lips.

"Wasn't a date," I started. "He just wanted to show me his old AP test material," I lied, hoping no one could see through me. But thank God Mom couldn't stop eyeing Jace so she didn't spare me a glance.

"God, why am I here?" Elaine muttered beside me, breathing out in exasperation.

"Shush," I told her as she kicked my foot under the table.

"You're not five."

She exhaled. "Mom, I need to fix my hair, I'll be in the bathroom," Elaine stated, before pushing me aside and practically running to the bathroom.

"Um... me too," I murmured, but neither of the two heard me, and I chased after Elaine because her hair was totally fine and I wasn't a dumbo. When I reached the bathroom, Elaine had two hands on both sides of the sink with her head down, I watched her chest rise up and down and her eyes were closed. She was breathing fast and hard, just as her fingers wrapped around the faucet, and I watched them tremble.

"Elaine..." I stared softly, walking towards her until I was right behind her. She didn't seem fazed by my showing up. She knew I would.

"I'm trying so hard to be okay with this. So hard. I feel like I'm living a lie. I'm not okay with it. It's too fast. I can't keep up with her, and then I remember the baby and I think we're going to have a step sibling, and Jace is going to move in and..." I cut her off, rapidly shaking my head.

"She's happy," I started, "I miss Dad too and Jace isn't going to be him. He's the baby's dad, not ours. Think of him as a support system. He wants to be there for you—"

"I want Dad," she interrupted swiftly, turning around as mascara took over her face.

"Elaine, *please* don't do this right now."

"I miss him."

"I know."

"No, you fucking don't, Ria. You weren't even that close to him—"

My face fell. "So? He's still my *dad*."

"But I was with him all the time. All the time. We went everywhere. We went hiking like every weekend. I would wake up earlier, like three times a week, to have breakfast with him before he left for work. I miss him and here's Mom giving no shit."

I couldn't argue with the last thing Elaine said. No matter how hard I tried to push that thought away, Mom really didn't care. She just wanted us to like Jace so it would be easier for him to move in faster. But that wasn't the problem. Liking him wasn't an issue. It wa*s missing Dad.* It was going into his office at home and not seeing him there. It was waking up at 1 a.m. and going down for a snack, to not see him watching Parks and Recreation. It was him being in family portraits hung all over the house, and me wanting to rip the photos and throw them in the trash.

But, instead of uttering a single word, I simply pulled Elaine into a hug as her body shook with tears that dripped all over my neck, but I didn't move. I didn't move until she did.

"When will I stop feeling like this?" she said into my neck, and I stiffened.

"That's a you thing."

"Will I ever?"

"Elaine, yes you will. I think we *kno*w what's happening but we haven't *comprehended* it all. And once you do, you'll stop feeling like that."

I grabbed a napkin with my free hand and she wiped at her nose and eyes.

"Come on," I murmured, weakly pulling her out of the bathroom as we walked back to the table.

We sat in the booth as if nothing happened and Mom looked at us as if nothing happened.

"We already ordered your meal, your favorite," Mom beamed, her cheeks pink and her face flushed. I didn't want to say anything so I simply bobbed my head up and down with the smallest smile tingling my lips.

We spent the rest of the night eating and talking about college and Jace's job. Mom was trying to get Elaine to talk more, but Elaine remained silent the majority of the time, only speaking when Mom brought up Brian. I tried not to say much, but Mom kept pulling me into the conversation, forcing me and Jace to talk again.

I ended up ordering dessert, just so I could distract myself and didn't have to talk as much.

* * *

Chapter Twenty-Six

"School's good! We haven't had it for the past week because of grading, but its good. How's Boston?" I asked Dad into the phone, hoping I could hear the smile in his voice when he talked. He chuckled and my heart warmed up.

"You should consider applying to Boston College."

I laughed. "I've heard really good things," I admitted.

"When do you think you're coming back?" I heard him sigh, like he was opening his mouth and then shutting it a second later.

"When I find a job there."

"Elaine misses you, a lot," I blurted, biting my lip as I waited for Dad to respond.

"I miss both of you. A lot."

"I love you. A lot," I murmured softly as Dad released a short laugh and I was hoping he was grinning.

"I haven't said that in so long and that's so wrong," I said.

"I haven't given you any reason to."

My lips twisted into a frown even though he couldn't see me.

"Stop," I muttered.

"Ria—"

"Don't. Don't say anything," I interrupted, lowering my voice even though no one was home.

"I love you," I said again, a smile lingering on my lips as I ended the call and leaned against the wall, clutching the phone to my stomach.

I went to school the following day and didn't talk to Flynn. And this happened for the next three days. I texted him once a day and he never responded. I knew something was up. I knew he was a senior and he probably wouldn't have even shown up to school, and God knew I didn't want to go there again.

So, after school, I drove to where I thought it was his house all along. I drove to the park, parked my car, and ran in the direction of where we always picnicked, with my head spinning. Part of me knew it was wrong. I knew he didn't want me at his house. I knew he didn't want me meeting his father. I never really pushed. I tried not to.

But I couldn't handle it. I couldn't handle three days without him. And I couldn't handle not knowing.

I walked down a pathway as I neared the white house. The stairs leading up to the door were crooked and falling apart, so I jumped onto the level, clearing my throat as my heart started frantically hammering in my chest, because I could hear *something* in the house.

I knocked on the door. I remember waiting for at least 10 minutes until the door swung open revealing Flynn, tears racing down his cheeks as his eyes went wide staring at me.

"Flynn—" My mouth was dry as he started frantically screaming.

"Ria, fucking leave. Get out. *Go home,*" he said, yelling as his voice continued to increase in volume.

"*Go home. Go home. Go home,*" he kept repeating, but his voice was strangled in his throat and then he suddenly screamed in pain, his arms instantly holding the side of his stomach. My heart had fallen onto the ground as I watched his eyes turn dark and tears continued to roll down his cheeks.

And then I saw a man in a wheelchair appear at the end of the short hall, his eyes wide as he started screaming.

"You retard, why the fuck would you open the door?"

Every part in my body was frozen and I just couldn't move.

I bent down towards Flynn but he pushed my hand away, waving his hands in the air frantically.

"Your girlfriend, huh, son?" The man said, slowly rolling down the hallway. His eyes were glistening with something unrecognizable, something that made my whole body start to shake.

"She's hot."

"Do—" Flynn tried to speak, but his voice was cracking with each sound.

"I could fuck her," his dad said with a laugh, and I looked away, feeling my stomach fall to the ground. I couldn't believe what I was seeing. What I was hearing. None of it felt like it was happening, but it *was*, and I couldn't do *anything*. Every limb and bone in my body was stiff.

"Don't you touch her like you do me." Flynn clenched his teeth together, growling. *Don't touch her like you do me.*

"She's easy if you can get her." The corner of his lips curled upwards into a small, teasing smile and it made my stomach squirm at the way he sounded. I felt like throwing up.

My voice felt like it wasn't in my control anymore. I remained still and silent because I just couldn't speak.

"Ria, get the fuck out." *Don't touch her like you do me. Does Flynn's dad? No. No. No. He wouldn't,* was all my head was saying.

"Flynn, I want you to leave," I said, with all my willpower.

Flynn's dad narrowed his eyes at me, darkness dancing in his pupils, and I shivered, not from the cold, but from his gaze. It was like I couldn't look away, but that was all I wanted to do. He was short, his hair the same color and style as Flynn's, but his eyes, green, and he looked at you a way no one ever had; a way that made my whole body tremble. A way that made my body shiver. A way that made me feel worthless and pointless.

"Get the hell out of my house," Flynn's dad yelled at me, rolling closer and closer towards me as I backed out of the door, my feet tripping on the doormat. *Don't touch her like you do me.* His hand wrapped around the sides of it before he slammed it shut, and I felt the wood beneath my feet rock and wobble. I remember banging on the door, repeatedly, until my knuckles hurt and were bruised and blood oozed out of cuts. I remembered I stood in front of his door for over an hour, begging Flynn to come out and leave, until my voice lost itself. I didn't understand what was happening, but I knew I didn't want him in that house. When the sun set, I stood up from my curled position against his front door and started walking out of the small lot, holding myself together. I screwed my eyes shut, hoping it was all a nightmare, and what I saw didn't happen, but I couldn't. Because every time I turned around and glanced at the house, my stomach flipped and my heart collapsed in my chest.

It happened.

I walked all the way home. All I wanted was to shut up and let the darkness succumb me, but his dad's words were the only thing running in my head and I couldn't get them out. *Don't do to her what you do to me.*

My hands were getting clammy and I couldn't find my thoughts or my voice. All I focused on was walking and getting home. *Home.* To Elaine and Mom, and to my bed. I called Flynn over ten times even though I didn't expect him to answer. I *still* called. I *still t*exted. I *still* left voicemails. I didn't even know what I was saying in any of the voicemails, my voice was barely audible and I was stringing sentences together that didn't make sense, hoping he could get the general idea of what I was saying.

He needs help and I couldn't do that for him, and that made me feel the way his dad stared at me. *Worthless. I couldn't help him. He couldn't talk to me.*

I reached a house to silence, except for mumbles I could hear upstairs. When I walked up the stairs, I was able to make out the voices as Mom talking to my dad. I couldn't make out much as their voices were basically inaudible and hushed.

"Yes, the kids are fine," she told him.

Fine.

The kids are fine.

We're fine.

I didn't even think Mom was paying enough attention to us to even be able to form that statement.

I dragged myself up the rest of the stairs, down the hall, and into my bedroom, where I, sadly, could still hear Mom and Dad's conversation as their voices grew increasingly louder with every second. I stuffed my face under my pillow, yanking the blankets over my body trying to get rid of their voices and their words. But my mom, dad's, and Flynn's dad's, were the only words I could hear, playing like a record in my head as I, eventually, drifted off into a slumber.

Part Two

THREE DAYS LATER

He wasn't answering.

I glanced at the number of messages left, and still, no response. I could feel my fingers beginning to shake as they glazed across his contact name in bright letters, and I released a breath I never realized I was holding. Liz told me to call the police and I did. I couldn't keep it to myself anymore.

God damn it. Where was he? I don't know where he is. *I don't know where he is.* I realized the sound of my heart rate increasing was a sign that I knew something utterly terrible was happening, but I couldn't pinpoint, exactly *what*. And that was by far the worst feeling imaginable. I suddenly felt the world was spinning on an entirely different axis as the numerous police cars came into view; the sound of a police car the only thing I could hear. I didn't understand what came over me; I hadn't a single idea of what was going on, but I felt like I *knew*.

So when the police entered my house without warning, I choked back a sob because the sheer sight of them worried me. *Where was he?* I started to move away to the corner of the room, lowering my body on the surface of the wood and yanking my phone out. I was crying before I realized it.

Eight days since our last texts. He read my message but never replied back. Everything flew into my head, the parties, the kisses, the dates, the dinners, the laughs, and it was then I realized, my head knew exactly what was happening but my heart refused to believe it. My fingers glossed across the texts messages, just as my head ached with a new pain that was unrecognizable.

It wasn't like this was the first time Flynn had been off the map; he had run away so many times that it almost felt normal. He never did anything like this when he was with me—was. *Was. Was.* The use of the word in the past sent an instant red sign to my chest. A *mess*. This is a mess. I was a mess. He was a mess. *This wasn't right.*

I guess the policeman understood something, because in an instant, he was racing up the sidewalk, pushing the front door open, and bombarding me with questions I had no response to. And that only scared me more because Flynn was someone I thought I knew, but maybe I didn't. Maybe I *never* knew. Maybe I created fake promises and fake people in my head to replace the true beings. Or maybe he simply never bothered to show me himself. All these months, I never truly knew him. And that hurt more than the idea of him being gone. Because he always was. Gone, gone, gone—my mind chanted as the policeman snapped his fingers in front of me in an effort to regain my attention, but maybe I was gone too.

"When was the last time you saw 18-year-old Flynn Johnson?" The police guy had an intent look in his eyes, his hand gripping a pen as he held a notebook in his other hand. He sighed.

"Henr—"

I couldn't look at him as I uttered my next words.

"*I don't know*. A week ago, I think. Maybe."

"*Maybe*? You're his girlfriend, correct?"

Girlfriend.

"Um…" I started, my voice drifting off into a mere whisper, and I hugged myself like I was cold, but only, I wasn't. *I was alone.* "Yes." The one word was supposed to roll off my tongue so smoothly, *yes, yes, yes, I was his girlfriend*, but it didn't feel like that and that wasn't right. I *should* know where he is. I *should* be there for him. I *should* understand him. Know him in ways he didn't. But I didn't. So I turned my body and started walking towards the front door, but the policeman caught up to me, his fingers gently brushing across the fabric of my tee.

"What's his house address?" And then I suddenly placed a hand to my mouth, covering the loud gasp as I hurriedly grabbed my car keys and ran off towards my car, leaving the man at my door with no response.

Oh God. My mind went into a whirl and I bit back a series of uncontrollable sobs that I knew would eventually crawl down my cheeks. I ignored my dad, my mom, my sister, and I just ran and the entire time, I prayed I wasn't right. He's not gone, I told myself. He wouldn't do that. He wouldn't do that to himself. To me. To *us.*

And then, in the back of my head, she whispered, *There hardly was*, and I couldn't even shake my head. In this state, I knew it wasn't even safe I was on the road, but I had to get to the barn before the police did. I racked my brain for the address as my fingers dug into the leather material of the steering wheel. Fuck, fuck, fuck, and then my eyes caught the smoke filling the sky behind his house—and it was *all I could see.*

Suddenly, everything froze.

I couldn't move, couldn't *breathe*, but only stared as the blue skies turned into a grey. And then, I was running—running towards the side of his house and forcefully pushing the backyard gate open as tears finally spilled across my lashes. I fell apart, as if my body was no longer in control of my actions. I couldn't feel *anything*.

"Fuck, *Flynn*! Flynn!" I covered my mouth, blocking the smoke as much as I could. And there, I saw, in the corner of my eyes, Flynn's dad's wheelchair broken in two, and his body laying still beside it, his eyes were wide open but his skin was pale. I couldn't look at him. I couldn't think about what happened or what Flynn did.

I could only think about *him.*

I tried to race around the barn, figuring out ways to enter. I couldn't see anything—everything was a dark black—until his curly hair came into view. He was here. *I was alone.* But he was here.

And then, I was falling to the ground; my trembling fingers snaking around his shoulders as I pulled and pulled him further and further from the burning barn. It was so hot. So dark. But I could still make out the pills surrounding his body.

"You're making a fucking mistake," I cried, gripping his left arm as forcefully as I could muster. I sucked in a harsh breath as my nails scratched into his white skin. It felt as if the only air I was breathing in was filled with utter poison; not that I really could breathe in anything.

Only mere seconds before, I couldn't see his chest rise up and down. Only seconds for me to feel the beat of his heart slow down, until it completely stopped and his body was perfectly and utterly still. *No. No. No.* I bent down, my fingers winding around his head as I furiously shook him. Over and over and over. I pressed at his stomach, his face, praying for a sound.

And then his eyes snapped open. And then he was begging for breath. His eyes grew as he grabbed my head, pulling me down towards him, but only, it wasn't *him.* It didn't feel like him; his hands pressed against mine; the touch felt different, felt fake; didn't look like him, because this boy laying in ashes in front of me, wasn't *my* Flynn. He was a *stranger.*

"Ria," he spluttered, coughing as blood came out from his nose and my sobs became the only sound I could make out.

30 MINUTES LATER

"Can I see him?" I was still shaking. I felt like my breath was sucked out of my lungs. My vision was blurry and my body was warm and hot. *Flynn tried to kill himself.* I shook my head. *He tried and he almost succeeded.*

The police officer shook his head, glancing at the ambulance.

"He's in critical condition. So is his father," he told me, and my face fell as I rubbed my hands together and a tear stung the corner of both my eyes, threatening to trip over my lashes.

"What happened to his father?" I asked, my voice so quiet, I was surprised he even heard me.

"I'm really not supposed to be telling you any of this, but he's dead." My mouth opened and I felt like throwing up when I remembered his body beside the wheelchair, and how pale his skin was and how lifeless he looked. *What happened?*

And the last thing I remember was being lead to the hospital, alongside someone I didn't know.

* * *

When I first opened my eyes, all I could see was light flashing into my eyes. I tried to stand up, but I couldn't, and it was then I realized I was in a hospital room, dressed in a gown and restless in the bed. I sunk into the pillow. I saw Mom, Jace, and Elaine, as I finally forced myself to sit up on the bed.

"What happened?" I asked, my voice hoarse from all the screaming. I was trying not to think about it. I didn't want to think about it.

"Oh my God, Ria, we couldn't find you. You passed out and..." my mom started, talking too fast for me to understand. So instead of uttering anything in return, I winded my weak arms around her neck and pulled her into a hug, pressing my face into the crook of her neck. Elaine stood behind her and I mustered a tiny smile.

"Where is he?" I blurted, standing up.

"He's in the room next to you. Only family can visit him." Elaine told me quietly, like she was afraid of talking to me.

"He doesn't even have any family," I grumbled, my fingers twisting around the edge of my gown.

"His dad?"

I shook my head, my gaze focused on the ground.

"What happened to him?" I asked my mom.

"He overdosed on pills." I ate the lodge in my throat, images of his body surrounded by pills filled my head, and I couldn't get them to leave.

"You should rest. They're going to let you leave in an hour," Jace finally said as I leaned back and sunk in the bed, dreams taking me away.

TWO WEEKS LATER

I ignored him.

Maybe if I just didn't say anything about that night, he would forget. *I* could forget. I couldn't believe I wanted him to forget about who I was. But I could not bear to look at him, knowing that I once liked him, after seeing what he wanted to do to himself. But, after what he did, he killed that. I felt my hands begin to tremble and suddenly images flew into my head. Ones of his life being sucked out of his pale body. Me crying. Me calling the police. Fuck, Fuck, Fuck.

He was in rehab and I was allowed to visit him, but I couldn't. I couldn't look at him the same. I couldn't look at him thinking about what he might have done to his dad. It wasn't just a coincidence. He did *something*.

I wanted to visit him, I did, but I knew for myself, I couldn't. He made me feel so many things. Half the time I wanted to kiss him until the air out of my lungs was sucked out, and the other half I wanted to stab him in the chest. We didn't argue. It was the silence that always bothered us. He was too sucked into his own feelings that he never bothered letting me know anything about crap.

I felt like a terrible person for feeling so angry.

I stay in front of my locker, still, as my hands wrapped around my anatomy textbook and I sauntered off to my next period. Liz came beside me, her hands snaking around my wrist as she whispered a series of words, but my mind was elsewhere and I couldn't even focus on anything she was saying.

"Visit him," she tells me, but I shake my head, the word 'no' rolling off my tongue so easily.

"Ria, why not? You want to know what the hell happened but you're not even going to see him?"

"I will. Soon. Just… I can't right now." I really can't. I can't look in his eyes the same way I did before. I can't go and press my lips to his the way I did before. I can't grip his hand and run my fingers in circular motions up and down his arm the way I did before. I can't talk to him the way I did before. Nothing's the same.

"He needs you. He lost his dad and you, right now, he needs someone he knows," she told me, but her words didn't faze me because I knew everything she was saying was true, but I just can't yet. I can't bring myself to go.

"I know," I tell her, my words coming out slowly as I grab my calculus textbook and walk to class.

"I didn't even study for the test," I grumbled. Fuck. I already have an 85 in this class.

"Just go home," Liz says, and I shake my head, my fingers grazing the frame of the textbook.

"I can't just *leave*."

She shrugs her shoulders. "Didn't stop you before."

My heart fell into a hole but I kept walking to class, not saying a word.

After school, Brian took me and Elaine home since Liz was going out to a movie with Jon. The car ride was silent. No one said a word to me like they were afraid. Elaine stared out the window, her hand molded with Brian's as he drove. I screwed my eyes shut because my dreams were always better than reality, and all I wanted was a chance to be *away*.

I called Dad the second I got home, like I was itching to hear his calming voice telling me it was all fine, and I would be okay, and Flynn would be too, and this would all end up just *okay*.

I didn't need perfect. Just okay.

He picked up on the first ring and I didn't wait a second to talk to him.

"Dad?" I said, like I was out of breath.

"Ria, Ria, honey I heard what happened and I was going to call you first thing, but I thought you needed space to breathe and just—" I cut him off.

"Don't apologize, Dad. I just need to talk to someone."

"What happened?" he asked me, and I inhaled before speaking.

"Dad, I found him. In ashes, surrounded by pills. I called the police and I guess my head exploded or something, because

I passed out and went to the hospital. I feel bad I haven't visited him in his rehab center, and I feel worse because I'm so angry with him and he almost died, and I just—"

"I can't believe you found him like that, but don't feel terrible for feeling like that. You have a right to be angry because you didn't know what was going on. But, Ria, you really should visit him soon."

I sighed. "Everyone keeps telling me that."

"What happened to his dad?"

"I..." I started, but my voice was hoarse and I didn't know how to say my next words.

"He died."

"*What*? Poor kid, he has no one. Ria, show him he has *someone*. He has you."

"He always did. I don't think he knew that," I paused. "I don't know if I ever even liked him, Dad. I mean, I thought he was cute, but I never knew him well enough to like him?"

My dad was silent for a bit.

"Just be his friend. He doesn't need a girlfriend. Just a friend right now." I bit my lip, remembering the way Flynn went crazy on me about needing a best friend.

"You're right." The corner of my lips lifted upwards into a short smile as I took in everything my dad said. I was glad Dad didn't ask anything in relation to Flynn's dad's death, because in the darkest part of my head, I had the slightest idea of what happened, but it wasn't something I could just say. It was too big of an accusation and it made me even more frightened of Flynn than I was before. I couldn't just ask him either. Maybe it was best I didn't know. I didn't *want* to know.

"Thank you, Dad, I love you. Visit soon."

"I just got settled with my job, I'll try in the next few weeks. How's your mom?" He asked the last part quietly, like he didn't want to but it slipped out anyways.

"Didn't you just talk to her?" I asked, referring to the week before.

"Wasn't much of a talk," he said, his voice low.

"What do you mean?"

"I mean, we spent the whole time arguing about..." he paused. He never finished the sentence.

"About what?"

"Nothing, darling. I have to get to work, my lunch break's over. I'll talk to you later, alright? Love you with my world." He didn't finish to let me say bye, which meant he was trying to avoid talking about whatever happened with Mom with me. And I didn't even mind. At this point, I was glad they divorced. I knew that didn't sound right, but the house felt like it was at peace and so did Mom, which I feel like I haven't seen since I was in middle school.

I thought about what he said. I was attracted to Flynn, that was a fact. But did I really, truly, like him the way I claimed I did? At times, I felt like I did. My stomach would flip flop and my heart would race when I saw him, and he was constantly in my head. But here I was, contemplating whether I even liked my boyfriend of four months.

I told him I loved him. I told him *lies* and I hated myself for it.

I slipped upstairs and collapsed on my bed, feeling my eyes become heavy already as I disappeared into a world of only my thoughts.

I had barely shut my eyes for thirty minutes as I heard the front door open and giggles filling the house. I turned and stuffed my face into my pillow, trying to cover my ears from the noise so I could sleep. Is it Elaine and Brian?

I walk down the stairs, and out of the corner of my eyes, I see Jace's hand up my mom's shirt, my mom's lips on his as Jace releases a guttural groan. My eyes grow as I instinctively cover my mouth and dash up the stairs, praying to God neither of them saw me.

What the fuck? They were about to fuck on the couch. I gagged at the mere thought, before eyeing the hallway again to see neither of them at the couch, and I sighed with relief before racing down the stairs. I saw my mom with Jace in Dad's old office. I didn't want to know what they were doing so I yelled out bye, not bothering to wait for a response and started walking to the cafe Liz works at.

It's similar to a Starbucks, as in, it has coffee but less expensive, because Starbucks costs five fucking bucks for a small frap, and I mean, who the hell can afford that? I feel my heart begin to hammer in my chest violently as I open the door to see a familiar face at the back of the room, his hands snaking around a coffee mug just as he turns around.

I can't tell if it's him or not, but I swear, once Flynn's eyes catch my face, *I fall and fall and fall.*

He slips me into his fingers and I can't seem to fucking get him out of my mind, and now I can't stop staring at his face. His eyes are a dark red, bloodshot even, and the bags under his eyes prove his lack of sleep.

And suddenly, I feel terribly sorry for him.

I want to run up to him, kiss him until I can't physically breathe, ask him what's wrong, and simply put, *I want to be there for him.*

But I find myself glancing away, my knees going weak and my hands turning a shade of white. I feel his gaze burn a hole through me and he begins taking long strides towards me, and my breath feels like its trapped in my lungs.

He walks towards me until he's only inches away, with a still face, and I feel my hands let go of the handle of my bag and I hear the sound of its thud as it lightly drops on the café floor.

"Henrietta," he merely whispers, coming closer and closer, and I don't even bother stopping him. I have so much to fix with him, *so* much to ask, so much to know, but in this second, I could give less than a flying fuck about anything because when he leans in and captures my lips in a searing kiss, I lose it all.

And then it hits me.

Fast and hard.

I find myself letting go and backing away just as my back hits the hard wall. I find the tears hitting my cheeks, and I find his face crushing. My fingers wrap around his elbow and I pull him out the café door so we stand beside the tables outside.

"What th—" I start, having a speech prepared, but I wasn't prepared for him to cut me off and say the words he did.

"I don't know how to say any of it. I…" he blurts, his hands carding through his locks with a sense of frustration.

"Just *try*," I whisper, feeling my fingers tremble and my lips still tingling from the kiss only seconds ago.

"I want to say I'm sorry, but that doesn't fix anything does it?"

He kept going, "My dad's gone."

My eyes softened and I wanted to cry for him.

"What happened to him?" I asked quietly, my voice barely audible.

"I know I owe you so many explanations. But first, I wasn't in the right state of mind when I…" He takes a deep breath, his voice turns quiet and weak. "Did what I did. I wasn't thinking, and I know that's not what you want to hear. *Fuck. Fuck.* I'm blabbering now, I can't seem to figure out how I want to say what I need to tell you, because I owe it to you to at least *tell you*. I felt like I was losing it. I didn't have Dad. Dad was threatening to not pay for my college tuition for the longest time, since I was maybe in the 6th grade. And he…" He pauses, taking in a breath. He never finished his sentence. "Then, there was the car accident and he lost his job and everything. I just felt like—"

"You had nobody and nothing," I finished for him, my voice low, yet thick with a sense of emotion.

"You always understand—" he starts, but I cut him, suddenly red all over and furious.

"*You fucking had me.* You had me, and you were that close to throwing me away. Do you not realize it? You *broke* me. I finally found someone I really really liked. I already lost my mom and my dad. I couldn't stand losing you, and I was *that* close to. You had me, and was that not enough? Fuck you," I finished, struggling to keep my voice leveled, and then he didn't say anything. I watched a single tear race down his cheek and my heart fell a bit, but I wasn't giving in.

"Really *liked*?" he asked, his voice quiet.

Oh God.

I look away, suddenly feeling redness crawl up my fingers.

"You never loved m—" he started, and I suddenly fell and wished I just never uttered those words, because I have no fucking idea what I feel towards him. He was first to notice me. First to accept me. First to see me, and maybe that's why.

He fucking broke my heart and I wasn't ready to give it back.

He already has it.

"I'm sorry," he finally whispered, ignoring his previous words, and I felt like slapping him even after what I told him.

"That's not enough." My voice was weak in my throat, feeling the tears hit my eyes. Fuck. Fuck. *I don't love you.*

"I'm trying. I got help. I needed it and I accepted that. I'm sorry for hurting you. I wasn't thinking, you have to understand, Ri—"

"*Don't* call me Ria." My teeth were now clenched and I choked back a series of sobs.

He swallowed. "*Ria*, I was sick. I get that's no excuse, but I never meant to hurt you."

"*But you did.*" My front lip quivered, my voice was fucking cracking and I felt so weak and so vulnerable breaking apart in front of him, but I needed him to know.

"Fuck you and your lies." My voice is laced with pure panic as I start running down the sidewalk so quickly, not realizing Liz was chasing after me, screaming my name.

* * *

I knew it was Liz at the door once I heard the pounding that seemed to never end against the cold wood. I stood still at the end of the hall, my breaths escaping quickly as I slowly made my way towards the front door. I could feel an ache spread through my arms, causing a slight shiver to race down my spine as I opened the front door with a face stained with tears.

"Oh, babe," Liz murmured softly, inviting herself inside as her small hands wrapped around my elbow, pulling me into the kitchen.

"You saw him, didn't you?" she asked me, her voice louder than before. And for a few seconds, I didn't answer because my mind was unable to process any words.

I begin to nod just as she releases a series of breaths and turns her head towards the window.

"What?" I ask, my voice inaudible and not realizing the words slipped out as if oxygen wasn't making its way in my lungs.

"What did he say?

"Exactly what I expected him to," I said, my voice barely above a whisper as I shoved my face into the palm of my pale hands.

"He's trying," Liz started, turning around as her eyes bored into mine, her blue orbs going dark.

I shrugged.

"*He is*," she argued, her voice nearing exasperation as she walked closer towards me and planted herself on one of the chairs from the table.

"I thought he was in rehab?" *This didn't make sense.*

"Maybe he didn't have a drug problem. Maybe he just took the pills to do it, and they got that."

"Maybe."

"You'll never know if you don't talk to him," she tells me.

I sighed, feeling my heart and head swell.

"I couldn't. I saw him and I don't know what happened, I just cracked. Like I was looking at some stranger. I couldn't do it," I murmured, my eyes on the ground.

"Give him a break," Liz finally uttered, and my head snapped up with enlarged eyes.

"A break? A *break*?" I repeated, my voice rising because I couldn't believe what it was she was saying, or at least trying to. I can't believe what I was saying. The words slipped off my tongue before I thought them through.

"God, Ria, this isn't *just* hard for you. It's hard for him too. I know he still likes you, and I'm positive you still like him too. At least he *came.* He's trying. Give him time to explain." Liz wrapped her arms around my neck, forcing me to indulge in a hug that I could not bring myself to return, simply because her words were on record player, repeating and repeating.

"You planned this?" I asked.

Liz nodded her head. "He needed to see you and you wouldn't meet him, so I just—"

I look away. "I told you I would." And I was going too. I just needed time the same way he did.

Liz looks at me with annoyance. "When, Ria? A month from now? He was your *boyfriend.*"

"We never even really broke up," I say quietly.

"Then there's a chance—" I cut her off because I knew what she was about to say, but I needed a break from i*t, him, all of it.*

"No. I want to be his friend. I want to help him. I just… it's hard seeing him, you know?"

"I know, babe, I know."

But she didn't. She didn't get it. I nod my head because my head wasn't functioning enough to form words and I just didn't know what else to say. My conversation with Flynn was still running in my head and I felt it ache. *Everything hurt.*

* * *

I walked home to an empty house, with a note saying Mom was at work because she forgot something, and Jace was stopping by later. I felt so angry I wanted to rip the note in half.

I release a sigh, just as my door opens revealing Elaine, her face lit with smiles and I stand up, forcing my lips to curl into a smile. But it's *Elaine*, and I know she notices my white face.

"Ria," she murmurs gently, and I simply shake my head.

"Don't." I grit my teeth looking at the carpet, and Elaine stares at me for a few more seconds before firmly nodding her head and explains Mom's here and I shake my head again.

"Please, Ria," she whispers, glancing down the hallway as if she were in panic.

"Let me help you the way you do me." *Don't touch her the way you do me.* Stop. *No.* Stop.

"No, I just need to study. I have a Calc test tomorrow," I said firmly, telling myself that and not her. I hadn't been focused on school for the past month and my grades were plummeting. Terrible timing considering it's a month before my junior year ends

"Why do you have to be like this? He survived, didn't he?"

"Yea, but we *aren't*," I whispered, the dreaded words burning my tongue as I said them aloud.

* * *

A day later, I checked the house calendar to see Mom had an ultrasound and growth appointment for the baby that morning. Something in me settled and clicked, and I found myself wanting to go to the appointment. Mom hadn't talked much about what happened with Flynn and his dad, and I think it's because the subject of the whole thing just makes her uncomfortable.

I thought she just didn't care, she didn't want to know how I was holding up. But I think she's trying to forget the whole thing and not let it affect us any more than it already is.

"Hey, Mom, is it okay if I tag along with you to the doctors?" She was rummaging around the kitchen, probably looking for the keys that I saw were on the table.

"Mom," I laughed. "Check the table."

She froze suddenly and turned around as her eyes met mine. She swallowed and dropped her purse on the ground.

"Wait, what did you say?" she asked, I could barely hear her. My brows furrowed in confusion as I glanced back at the table with the keys.

"The car keys—"

She shook her head. "No, about the appointment."

My lips turned into a grin. "Can I come with you?" I repeated, slower this time as her whole face broke into a smile and she rapidly nodded her head.

"That would be wonderful."

I chuckled, excited to see the baby in the cameras.

We drove together in a silence that was liked, and wasn't awkward or strange. There was no need for a conversation. I simply gripped my mom's hand like she was a little girl and smiled the whole way. I hadn't felt so happy in so long.

We wait in the waiting room as a lady calls my mom's name. I watch my mom get her ultrasound done and I see the baby in the screens.

"Oh my God, Mom," I murmur, staring at the screen with my palm attached to my mouth and my smile growing with each second.

She gripped my hand. "It's beautiful, right?"

"Stunning," I say with a grin. I never thought about the fact I would be getting a sibling out of all this and that got me so excited. Somehow, a good thing came out of every bad thing.

"The baby looks healthy and is following the pattern," the doctor writes in her notebook with a smile. "Just keep taking care of yourself," she tells my mom as I help my mom sit up.

"You're lucky to have a daughter who seems like she's gonna be a great older brother or sister," the doctor said looking at me, and I turned red glancing at the wall.

"I really am. She's the best," my mom said, and I felt my heart twist the right way.

"That was so cool," I say as we leave the room.

"Come more often," my mom answers with a smile as we leave the doctor's office. I grab her hand and nod my head.

TWO DAYS LATER

I'm third-wheeling with Jon and Liz, and they're out shopping while I sit at a nearby coffee shop, waiting for the two love birds. It's late in the day, about 8 p.m., and the mall is about to close anyway. Dad was at home and Elaine was with her boyfriend, Brian, at the movies.

Seeing Liz with Jon made me smile and happy to see that not all relationships fall apart. Some, can work. Unlike Mom and Dad. Some last.

My fingers snake around my phone as I open up the word application and have a quick revision for my AP US HISTORY exam tomorrow.

Liz and Jon come up, as I can hear the two laughing and I am taken back to two nights ago with Mom and Dad. I drown on the memory for a second, and then decide it's best to forget, and I lift myself up and smile.

"Find anything?" I ask, lopping my arm around Liz just as Jon sneaked a kiss.

"You two can't be without each other for a sec," I laughed, and Jon's lips curled into a smirk as he looked at Liz.

"Yea, well, she can't stay away."

"Neither can you," I add, my eyes gleaming, and Liz's face breaks into a smile as she presses her lips to Jon and I fake a gag just as she wraps his around his neck.

I can't stay away. I can't stay away.

"Always PG, guys."

"R in the bedroom," Jon mutters, and I swat him, disgusted as Liz's face turns red. But she whispers something into his ear, causing Jon to suck in a breath and a redness filled his cheeks. I laugh again, and me and Liz walk ahead of him as Jon shakes his head the whole time, muttering a string of curses.

Once I arrive home, Elaine pulls me into a sudden hug and my shopping bag drops to the floor. She clutches me so tightly, as if she's afraid this is the last time she's going to see me. I pull away, a soft smile pulling at my lips as she stares at me with small eyes.

"What's wrong?" I ask her, confused and motioning to the hug; it wasn't the hug that confused me, it was her face.

"Nothing… I just wanted to hug you. I've missed you," she mutters, and I feel terrible and I find myself pulling her into one more hug, pushing my head into the crook of her neck.

"How's Brian?" I asked her, a smirk playing on my lips.

She turned around, her face a bright red and she rapidly shook her head.

"Shut up!" She pointed towards the hallway, her face going white, and I laughed again. Didn't she just hang out with him?

"Elaine, were you not *just* out with him at the movies?"
She shrugged.

"Hey, Brian!" I yell, my body vibrating with laughter, and a young brown-haired boy appeared at the end of the wall and Elaine shook her head, eventually releasing a laugh, and we drowned in the beautiful sound.

* * *

11:52 p.m.

Brian left an hour ago, and me and Elaine played Uno for a bit before I decided to go to sleep, even though I knew I wasn't going to be able to. I told Elaine it was okay when she asked if I wanted to sleep with her. I loved how she finally *understood*. I was strangled between numerous blankets on my bed as I wrapped my fingers around my phone, swiping to the left.

It suddenly vibrated and my fingers glazed across the screen. I raked the screen, my bottom lip suddenly trembling.

11:54: Flynn <3: iaiuwwiwidhu drunk
11:54: Flynn<3: im so sorry ria
11:55: Flynn <3: huwsje i still like you
11:55: Flynn<3: i still cant believe i did what i did
11:57: Flynn <3: i love you. Im sober and i I love you. my dads gone. ur all i have.
11:57: Flynn<3: im so sorry for hurting you
11:59: Flynn <3: i miss us.

And then:

12:00: Flynn <3: im here now. i wont be going anywhere. not like before.

Flynn, I don't know if there ever was an *us*. I couldn't handle reading the messages about his dad. His dad was dead. His dad was gone. And I couldn't imagine what he was feeling. Even if his relationship with his dad was screwed over from the beginning, he was always present, maybe never *there*, but present, and he was just *gone.*

Chapter Twenty-Seven

After getting ready for school, I trudge down the stairs.

I remember reading Flynn's texts.

I still like you.

I miss us.

I'm sober and I love you.

Does he even know what love is? Because I don't. And I don't know what I feel anymore. My head hurts at the mere thoughts, and for a fleeting second, I wonder what it could feel like. I was fucked for my English test. I didn't even read the chapter, but I just couldn't think about anything other than him and his dad, and rehab, and seeing him that day. I wanted to ask him what was wrong. I did. I want to help him, talk with him, be there for him. I always was, but he never realized that.

Without really thinking, I grabbed my phone and texted him.

Me: Are you in rehab?

He replied in a second.

Flynn: I never had an addiction.

Me: What's going on?

Flynn: My dad's dead.

I inhaled a breath because I didn't know what to say to that.

Flynn: *Is it bad I feel so relieved?* I released a sharp breath. I needed him to tell me.

Flynn: Come over, please.
Me: Okay.

I couldn't say no and I couldn't keep ignoring him. I had to remember everything that happened before. I had to understand this was always him and I just didn't know, and now I needed to let myself in and let myself finally *know.*

When I arrived at his house, I pushed away all memories of what happened here and continued to just walk up the stairs as I knocked on his door. I stood there for at least 20 minutes. No one responded and I felt sick to my stomach. Like the feeling I had when the police came to my house.

I take out my cell, pressing his contact name, shakily pressing my cold cell to my ear. "Please, *please* answer," I whisper to myself, and then the line rings and rings and rings, and then there's only the sound of someone breathing. Fast and hard. And it suddenly stops, replaced with a deadly silence.

"Flynn?" I ask, my voice hardly audible.

It hangs up.

* * *

I left him 12 messages and four voicemails, but he still hasn't responded to anything. I feel sick. I press a finger to my temple, struggling to breath. In. Out. In. Out. In. Out. In. Out. It's 8:34 p.m. and I can't think straight.

Maybe that's because I'm surrounded by drunk men and women at a bar; a vodka wrapped around my hands as I bring it to my lips, swallowing more. *Forget. I want to forget. Forget. Forget everything.* I wipe my lips, clumsily buttoning the top button of my dress because it keeps popping.

I came alone, but there's a man who keeps asking me to dance, but I'm not drunk enough to agree to it. I can't do that to myself. But, I call Flynn again. My hot breath fanning over the phone as I struggle to say the words that can't form in my head.

"I—" I start, and then he talks, and I feel the world halts, leaving only me and him.

"I'm coming," he murmurs, and then ends the call and I fall a bit in my seat, clutching the phone to my chest.

I wait 10 minutes or so, all fidgety in my seat. I can't think or move, or... *What the hell is going on?* My head is throbbing, my heart is throbbing, but I keep sitting on the stool. Waiting and waiting, even when so many people keep yelling and the music is so loud I fear I will go deaf. And then I see him enter, and his eyes scan the room just as they land on me.

I know I'm smiling like a lunatic, my face breaking into everlasting, wide smiles. And I can't stop. Because I don't *want* to. He comes up to me, taking in my sight, and I poke him in the chest, tugging him towards me as close as I can because I fucking never want to let go.

"It's my turn now," I whisper leisurely, and clutching his neck, I press my lips to his. He tastes sweet. Soft. As good as he always had. As if it was the first time I kissed him. *It feels like that.* And I feel his hands tingle my waist, and I feel my hands loop around his neck. And I feel warm and red all over. But I can't stop.

"You're drunk," he states as he pulls away, and I am sure my breath smells terrible, and I'm sure I'm a horrid kisser since it's been so long, but he's not one to tease me of that.

I quickly nod.

"I am... so... very drunk." I give him a lazy smile, and he looks at me with confused eyes that my mind suddenly accepts.

"Ria, what's happened?" He asks me, his voice sincere and quiet. His eyes rake my dress and I watch him swallow before his cheeks turn the lightest shade of pink. I find myself laughing.

"You happened," I answer, the word slipping from my tongue without me thinking.

He looks hurt, and suddenly, I feel bad again.

"Fuck," I whisper, my voice hardly audible and the word was meant only for my ears, but I know he heard it.

"I still like you," I blurt, my words coming quickly before I can process what it is I'm saying. "I don't want to, that's the issue. I want to hate you, I do, but then you kiss me and *fuck,* then I kiss you and I just am afraid of… of… of… **swallows** losing you again. I don't know if I can handle it. I don't know what this feeling is. *I don't know,*" I rush blabbering, and then I finally glance up, ready to take in his expression.

He kisses me again. Quick and hard.

"Ria, I don't know if—" he starts, and I feel my chest twist and turn at what he may say.

"Please. Just for now. Nothing else," I whisper, grabbing his hand and molding it with my own as I hastily move up the stairs of the bar.

"Ria," he tries again, his breath fanning my ear, and I swallow, turning to face him.

"Please, I can't take it anymore." I try to latch my hands around his neck, but he slowly takes them off and I look away; my heart drops.

"You're drunk," he says again, his voice firm and cold, as if he's mad at me.

"I know," I say.

"I can't, Ria. I can't do something like this when I know you would never say this when your sober," he says, his voice strangled in his throat. His hands begin carding through his locks in anger as his eyes meet mine, and I move back a step.

My vision went black and I screwed my eyes shut as I tried to escape from him. I could feel the bile in my throat, the tears at my eyes, and I was falling apart. I clutched my head, and everything fell back into me, and I hated that I was breaking in front of him.

"Ria," he called for me, but I was moving away.

Why did I do this?

"No, no. You're right," I said shakily, my voice leaving me, and I held myself.

"Ria, I don't want to hurt you like that. I was hurt by my dad, in ways you won't ever want to know, and I just don't want to drag you into it again." *Stop. Stop, Flynn.*

"What are you trying to say?" My voice went quiet, and I finally brought myself to look him right in the eyes; mine turning black.

"I... I..." Before he could respond, I get out my phone, swipe to the left, and shove the phone in his face so he can read the text messages he sent me. Does he not remember?

"What about these?" I sarcastically laugh, just as his hand snaked around the cell and his eyes went wide.

"I didn't mean to send you those," he said, his face paled and that gave it all away. The blood drained out of his face and I laugh again. Laugh and laugh. Over and over. I feel powerful, strong, and terrible, but I love it.

Oh yea. "*I like you. Still. I won't leave again. Not like before.*" I read, my head pounding and my body vibrating with sarcastic laughter. I snatch the phone from him, continuing to read his texts aloud.

And then his face breaks.

"Stop, stop. Ria. *Stop*," he rasps out, dragging his words.

Then, I find myself nodding my head, finally whispering a few words I've wanted to say since I saw him tonight.

"Then *why*? Flynn, I just want some explanation, I want to know what happened, I want t—"

"Oh fuck, Ria, I can't tell you. *I can't*," he shouts, and I fall to the ground, holding myself as tight as I could but never looking back.

"Then don't," my tone is soft but firm, and I hope he knows I'm doing this for him. I don't want him to hold it in anymore. I know how it feels, leaving everything to your own head, and it hurts when you think no one's going to listen, but, Flynn, someone's always there. You can't hold it all in.

Communication is key, were Flynn's words. Once. Feels like it was in a different world, during a different time, when he once uttered those words. But, they're so very true and I hope he still sticks by it. *Tell me. Talk to me. Please.*

He rubs at his forehead and looks down at me with a sharp and intent gaze that I can't look away from.

"It's my dad," he finally murmurs, and I nod my head because I guessed that, but my heart picks up as I watch his face change.

"What did he do?" I ask, my front lip trembles as I ask those words. I don't know if I'm ready to hear his response because I know his dad. I had just seen him and I couldn't bear the thought that Flynn had to live with that man.

Flynn remains silent, not answering as he turns his head and sits down on the ground so he is directly opposite if me. He opens his knees, pushing his face between his legs. I don't realize for several seconds that his entire body is shaking as he looks up. His breath grazes my face, and soon, it's not 'just him trembling in the dark.

"I can't bring myself to say it," he finally says, and I begin to find his hand in the dark and lock my fingers with his.

"It's okay. It's okay to *not* be okay," I speak softly, the truth in my words hit me in the chest. I don't know what we are. I don't know if there ever will be an us again. But in this second, I could care less, because Flynn wasn't okay. And what mattered was helping him, so maybe he could be *okay* again.

And then, we sat in the darkness as sobs began to rip through Flynn's body, and he clutched my hand so tightly, it went red. I moved my body so I sat beside him. Our knees touched. I looked at him, as if I was asking permission to place my head on his shoulder, but then I just did. My breaths went steady but his didn't as he cried in my arms, and this time, I held him in hopes he understood my actions.

Chapter Twenty-Eight

I wake to the sun shining in my face, but to a different bedroom than the one I sleep in at home.

And, I don't feel surprised, I feel somewhat dizzy, and that's when my head painfully throbs and I clutch it, only hoping that takes the painful ache away for a second. I look beside me only to see an arm is draped across my waist. I know this is Flynn's bedroom, and I feel my heart race when I realize he's shirtless and the elastic of his boxers are showing from the bed covers. I know he sleeps that way, but it feels different when *I'm* in the bed beside him. I notice my dress sleeve has fallen off, my bare shoulder in view.

I take this second to drink in the sight of his face. He's snoring, very quietly, and then suddenly, he secures his arm around my waist and pulls me flush against him.

I know a small gasp escapes my lips, but his touch is so warm and my face is directly below his chest. *Bare* chest.

Oh damn. But then, I look down towards the right end of his chest and there's the smallest cut on his waist, and I suddenly remember. It's stitched, and so small, one can hardly see it, but it's there in my eyes, and I suddenly feel like crying for him. I remember. *Oh God, it's not what I think it is.* I won't know anything until he tells me something.

"Flynn," I whisper, but he doesn't move or make a sound.

What the hell happened last night? I'm praying I didn't do anything stupid. I remember showing him those texts, and I remember him sobbing. I don't remember how I got to his house and why the hell my dress sleeve is ripped.

Mom's going to hurt me, I'm already not on good terms with her, but there's some improvement, I suppose. I shouldn't be here. I can't do this, not yet. I don't know if I'm ready. I keep waiting, but I have no damn idea what it is I'm waiting for? I stare at the young boy, whom I *believe* I very much like, and I wonder. And wonder. I slip myself off his bed, careful to not wake him as I stand in front of the door.

"Before you say anything," I start, coughing. "Please, put a shirt on," I tell him, and his eyes gleam with amusement and, fuck, I haven't seen him smile and sparkle like he is, and I know my face is filling with smiles.

"I think I like this better, and so do you." His lips tug into a smirk, and I groan at him. He stares at me, and I look away, embarrassed by the way I look. I don't understand why I always feel nervous of my looks when he's around. He always made me feel beautiful and I don't know why that's changing. The room turns silent before I speak.

"I can't focus with you like that," I say truthfully. Suddenly shivers crawl down my back, my face, my hand. His lips begin to graze my jaw, and he peppers a series of kisses down my neck. I feel a shiver crawl down my back and I know I'm turning pink and red, and I don't even care because it feels so good.

Distraction. He's distracting me.

"Flynn."

He continues, his arm wrapping around my waist.

"You smell like strawberries," he whispers, his voice muffled and raspy from the morning. I back away and his eyes darken as he stares at me again. I remember what happened last time he looked at me like that, and my heart flips in my chest.

"Flynn," I breathe again, as if he was a dream that vanished from my memory. "Yea?" he murmurs gently, and I look up to him, my eyes meeting his as he swiftly presses a kiss to my cheek. He deliberately hasn't touched my lips yet, and I don't want him to. Not yet, at least.

"Don't ever wear this dress again," he says, his voice slow and uncontrolled. I laugh, because I don't know what else he wants me to do.

I throw his shirt and a pair of pants at him.

* * *

Flynn walks to the bathroom and he leaves me to sit on his bed. I carefully pull the blankets together, my mind hazy as I flash back to sleeping beside him. I hadn't slept that good in ages. I gripped the edge of the pillows and pulled them together. Satisfied, I planted myself on his desk chair, waiting for him to come out.

I see a small notebook on his desk and I latch my hands on it.

But before I can even see what it is, the door opens, revealing a wide-eyed and a slightly paled Flynn.

"Ria," he spluttered, making three quick strides towards the desk I was now standing in front of. I didn't get a chance to read it, but something tells me he didn't want me to.

"Hey, I haven't done anything," I say, but it doesn't change his face.

"I don't even remember what I wrote in that," he says. It's a journal.

"Here," I hand it to him.

He shakes his head.

"No, you should read it. If I want anyone to, it's you."

"Flynn…" I start, but he shakes his head again as he moves to sit on the bed. My bottom lip shakes as I open it and read the first page.

"It's in bullets," I state quietly, and Flynn nods.

I ignore the words and see there's no date on any of the pages.

> – *it hurts more than I thought it would.*
> – *I'm pretty sure he dislocated my shoulder.*

My face falls as I read the last sentence again and again.

"Who's *he?*" My bottom lip trembles as I speak so quietly, afraid to speak any louder.

"You know," Flynn says, his gaze focused on the book in my hands.

I swallow before flipping the page.

> – *I tried painting the house.*
> – *he got mad.*
> – *he did it again.*

"I can't say it," I whisper, as he looks down.

"Don't say anything."

> – *my stomach is purple*
> – *I don't want to look at him*
> – *he'll hide the food again.*

"Hide the food?" I swallowed again, my fingers shaking around the paper.

"He didn't," I stated, shaking my head rapidly back and forth and shutting the journal. I stared at Flynn, my eyes growing.

"He didn't."

"I didn't know why," Flynn said quietly. "I wasn't a bad kid. I did almost everything he asked. I skipped school to help him. I've missed so many days, I was so behind on everything all for *him.*"

"Flynn." My voice was caught in my throat and I feared if I spoke anymore I would cry.

"He told me I couldn't go to college. I had to stay with him. Even with that, I thought what was the point? I was going to live the rest of my life taking care of my dad and working at his car shop." Flynn laughed. The one that hurt your ears.

"*What was the point?*" he said again. He threw his head back. "I wanted to go to school, he hit me and locked me in the basement. We had no money. I started selling drugs. It made money quickly and I would go and buy food with it. I needed some way to get things. Dad couldn't go on his own." He paused, a smile on his lips. The one that hurt your eyes.

"And the funny part of this whole thing? I would bring food. And he would hide it. Like he was five. He threw me in the basement and didn't feed me. Remember when I came over? After I said sorry. I hadn't eaten anything in three days." I tried to say something, but he interrupted and kept talking.

"What the fuck was the point? I hated being in my own house. I couldn't go anywhere. I couldn't go to college. I couldn't do anything. I was worthless. I was failing school because I was barely there. They wanted to expel me. But Dad *wouldn't let me go."*

"I wanted out… of all of it. I couldn't be what you wanted. I couldn't give you a future, I couldn't be good for you. I was

a mess and I didn't know..." he paused, breathing out. "What to do."

"I wanted to stop thinking. I wanted it all to stop spinning."

I sat on the ground because my knees were breaking on me.

I swallowed. "Did you ever, ever..." I breathed out. "Complain or report him?"

"I tried. That day you saw me at the police office. I tried, but I couldn't. The bruises looked like I fell and my dad would deny it."

"You didn't want me touching you that day. You didn't want me at your house. You would disappear," I started, my thoughts slipping out of my lips before I could stop them.

"I never pushed. I should have pushed it out of you, I wish I could have help—"

"He's gone. He's dead," Flynn murmured. "He can't do anything anymore."

"What did he do?" My voice was quiet and my words were coming out slow.

"He overdosed on his medication for his legs. He's gone."

Flynn remained silent, and then, he lifted his shirt. Throwing it to the floor as his finger pressed against the smallest cut, caressing it. And I could only stare with a falling heart. "This one was the worst. He was drunk when I came home. I told him I did well on my SAT's and I told him I needed to go to college." He swallowed, and a tear rolled down my cheek because I couldn't stand knowing this, and I couldn't stand looking at him.

"You were about to die," I whisper, failing my hands around my body as I slide down the wall and land on the floor. I clutch my body, holding myself, afraid to lose myself.

"And you don't think I wanted to tell you? If Dad..." He looked away, his throat clogging with tears as his voice turned quiet. "I couldn't tell you; didn't want this to change how you felt. I knew you would have felt sorry for me, maybe forced yourself to like me more than you did, out of pity. I also didn't want that. I wanted your feelings real. I've never cared more about someone than you," he finally said, and I felt my hands curl into fists. Because he could have. And there was so much I could have done to help him, and be there for him, and make his dad fucking stop.

"You cared about my fucking feelings over what your *dad was doing?*" Flynn, that's, that's just not righ—" I paused, watching my words because I was scared to say something that wasn't right. Flynn didn't say anything. And I finally see it, I finally understand it. "Oh, Flynn," I spoke softly, so softly my voice was barely above a whisper as I moved closer to him. And then he lifted his hand in the air, and I stumbled back into his desk chair.

"Ria, I keep hurting you—" he started, and I knew exactly what he was about to say. I stood up, my breath grazing his face as I furiously uttered my next few words.

"Don't you dare tell me you're no good for me. That's for me to decide. Not you." Instead of saying anything else, I latched my arms around his neck and pulled him into a hug, his tears wetting my shirt as I pressed my lips to his neck and remained still. I didn't want to leave him. I didn't want him here alone. And in that second, I looked up and I saw *my* Flynn, for the first time since I met him.

Chapter Twenty-Nine

"Stay with me," I mumbled into his shirt and he stiffened, lifting his head up.

"My aunt's taking me in. And she also signed me up for therapy sessions, and I haven't gone yet," he says.

"When?"

Flynn looked away. "My first one was today." My lips turned into a frown and he notices my reaction and swiftly presses his finger to my lips.

"I'll go when I want to talk. You go home," he says, and I nod my head because I don't want to utter anything else.

"You sure?"

He nods his head. "I'm sure. I'll just watch a movie and sleep on the couch. I'll text you." I don't hug him or kiss him as I leave, I simply smile and wave my hands before gently shutting his door and walking home, suddenly feeling a void in my chest as I leave.

* * *

When I get home, I run into Elaine at the door.

"You saw him?" she asks me with a sad smile, and I nod my head, gripping her hand. Her gaze lowers.

"How is he?"

I scoffed, "How do you think?" Her face falls and she starts to move her feet and I roll my head back. I didn't mean it to come out like that.

"I didn't—" She shakes her head, something in her eyes, something bright.

"How are *you?*" she asks me quietly, and I find myself not answering for at least a minute. I didn't know what to say. There were so many things, and some things made no sense, and there were still holes in my head that I didn't think could ever be filled. Instead, I let myself smile as I walked past Elaine.

"I'm okay," I finally murmur, the use of the word finally making sense to me. *I'm okay. Flynn's going to be okay. And we're all going to be okay.* Not perfect. But okay was good enough.

"Mom's inside," Elaine says as she gets in my car, and I nod my head, not turning around and not speaking, because I feel a lump grow in my throat and I didn't know why.

I walk in and Mom's there, and she runs towards me as her hands wrap around my shoulders and she brings me close— just holding me. The way she held me as a child. And I didn't want her to let go. I put my head on her shoulder and just stood there, lightly breathing.

She didn't need to say anything. Her presence was enough.

"You saw him didn't you," she states and I move back.

"He was a mess, Mom. He made me a mess."

She ruffles my hair. "You always were one." I swat her arm, a grin growing on my face. I find my hand landing on her tummy and my mom giggles.

"I'm happy for you," I say.

"You coming to that appointment meant the world."

"I'll come to the gender one too," I say, and her face breaks into a smile and I laugh, snaking my arms around her waist and just holding her.

"You have every right to still be angry with me. I'm never going to forget I was the main reason for the split, just the cherry on top. But I want you to know your dad just wasn't happy anymore. I didn't know what to do. He tried to make it work, we both did, but sometimes it just doesn't work. Love can stop."

"Mom, you don't need to explain anymore," I tell her, mainly because I just can't hear about this anymore, their relationship's gone and Jace is here.

"I feel like I always need to," she mutters, and I laugh sitting with her on the couch.

"Ria, I want you to help him. Please help him. Be there for him. You don't have to date him, no matter what he wants, but be there for him. He needs someone. He has no family. And I'm beyond sorry I acted as if we never were one." My mom blurted those words I wanted to hear for so long and I finally have. So, I hugged her again, and I didn't want to let her go, and I didn't want to ever leave. I clutched the hem of her T-shirt and she pulled me as close, and I stayed like that for hours.

TWO WEEKS LATER

"Are you ready?" my mom yells from the hall downstairs as I look in the mirror and straighten out my black dress. I pull my hair into a bun and start walking down the stairs. It was Flynn's dad's funeral today. His aunt set it up and I didn't even know if Flynn was going to attend. No one really knew.

Elaine, Jace, my mom, and me, all get in the car and I drive to the church.

We get there and its filled with people I hadn't seen before. But my eyes are only focused on the coffin in the front, and images of his body, lifeless, surrounded by smoke and pills fill my head, and I screw my eyes shut. I breathe out, eyeing the room for Flynn, but I can't find him.

I end up sitting down on one of the benches, with my head down and gaze focused on my black shoes, because I can't look at the coffin. I feel sick. I hold my stomach.

The ceremony ended quickly. Flynn never showed his face. I went off to the bathroom and I heard someone in the men's room, and my heart fell because I just *knew*. I had heard him cry so many times. But I had something else in mind when I walked in and I saw him, leaning against a stall with tears dripping down his cheeks.

I held out my hand. I knew I couldn't say anything in that moment that would help him. I can't say I know how it feels. Sorry fixes nothing. I just wanted to be there. He has someone.

He has since he drove me from the bar that night.

He glances up and wiped at his face, his tears gone in a second, like they were never there.

"Hi, I'm Ria. You?" I smile, as his lips curl into a smile and he shakes my hand.

"I'm Flynn," he says.

* * *

CPSIA information can be obtained
at www.ICGtesting.com
Printed in the USA
LVHW080214290619
622760LV00032B/458/P

9 781641 829052